ROBERTA LEIGH

an impossible man to love

Harlequin Books

TORONTO • NEW YORK • LONDON
AMSTERDAM • PARIS • SYDNEY • HAMBURG
STOCKHOLM • ATHENS • TOKYO • MILAN

Harlequin Presents first edition April 1988
ISBN 0-373-11066-9

Original hardcover edition published in 1987
by Mills & Boon Limited

Printed in U.S.A.

CHAPTER ONE

'I'M DAMNED if I'll have a woman architect working on my Clinic!'

Stephanie Rodgers stared disbelievingly at the Savile Row-suited man behind the desk, unable to credit that anyone with a Western education could say such a thing.

'I thought Turkish women were emancipated, Mr Hamid,' she said in a carefully controlled voice.

'Depends what you mean by emancipated,' came the reply. 'Well educated, yes, and many professions are open to them, but as in all things, Miss Rodgers, one cannot discount personal prejudice. And mine is not to work with a woman.' The look he gave her from deep-set, dark eyes couldn't be described as anything other than hostile. 'I refuse to believe a firm like Lister and Young didn't have a man for the job.'

'Of course they did!' Stephanie exclaimed. 'But I've worked on this project with Mr Lister from the start.'

'Is that so?' he said insolently.

'Yes, that *is* so,' Stephanie bit out each word. 'I've been here twice with Mr Lister, but you were abroad so we didn't meet, and when he had his accident, he thought it logical for me to take over from him.'

'Logical it may be—acceptable it isn't,' came the rejoinder, and it was all Stephanie could do to control her temper.

Had the company been hers, she would have told this arrogant Turk exactly what he could do with his damned project! But she was only an employee—albeit a trusted one—and the Clinic to be built in memory of Mr Hamid's father was too lucrative a commission to lose.

Yet it hadn't entered her head—or John's either—that their client would object to a female architect. After all, this was the nineteen eighties, and he an educated, travelled man of the world. Added to which, from what she had seen of Turkey, there was a definite juxtaposition of the old and the new: black-garbed women, their faces hidden behind the veil, rubbing shoulders with mini-skirted girls out strolling with their boyfriends, or serving you with total freedom in shops and restaurants.

Little wonder she had assumed the country to be well on its way to taking its place in the Western world, and forgotten that Kemal Atatürk—the visionary who had prodded Turkey into the twentieth century—had said, 'Remain yourselves, but learn how to take from the West what is indispensable to an evolved people'.

Well, it now looked as if one of the things certain Turkish businessmen *hadn't* taken from the West was female emancipation! Stephanie bit back a sigh, silently acknowledging she hadn't reckoned on the reactionary views of men like Tariq Hamid, who wanted his women subservient, allowing them freedom only as long as it didn't infringe on his liberty and life-style. And from the look on his face as he stared at her, she was one threat he intended getting rid of!

'Whether or not you like me being in charge,' she stated, meeting him stare for stare, 'the work has to be completed.'

The man leaned back in his chair, placed his fingertips together and silently focused on a point above her head.

Surreptitiously, from beneath long, thick lashes that needed no mascara, she studied him. *His* lashes were long too, extraordinarily so for a man, and framed eyes as black and glittering as jet. Hair, of the identical colour, was lightened by a sprinkling of grey at the temples—though he could only be in his mid-thirties—and sprang away from a high forehead. Undeniably a handsome man, she conceded, despite the fact that his olive-skinned face with its perfect features was marred by a disagreeable expression that gave a thin-lipped harshness to a mouth that ordinarily would be beautifully cut and sensuous.

Stephanie waited patiently for him to speak, and had concluded he was going to ignore what she had said, when he commented drily, 'You're right, Miss Rodgers. The Clinic has to be finished.'

'So you agree to my taking over from Mr Lister?'

'There doesn't seem to be an alternative—for the moment.'

For the moment. It was only a temporary reprieve, Stephanie knew, and realised she had no recourse but to accept it. Besides if she proved herself capable of taking over from her senior partner, this arrogant Turk might have the grace to forget his prejudices and leave her in charge. It would create problems for their firm if he didn't, for only she and John knew the difficulties that could arise during the construction of this building.

'Then it's settled, Mr Hamid,' she said tonelessly.

'Temporarily,' he reiterated. 'And only because I don't want any delays.'

'Nor do we. When Mr Lister broke his leg and knew he——'

'Broke his leg?' Thick, black eyebrows came together in a straight line above the long, narrow nose. 'I hadn't realised it was so serious.'

'Not serious,' Stephanie put in quickly. 'You can always get him on the telephone. It's simply that he'll be immobile for the next few months.'

There was another silence, and the eyebrows became twin arcs above the heavily lidded eyes. Then impatiently the man rose, indicating the meeting was over. Seated at his desk, his raw masculinity had been partially disguised by his impeccably tailored suit; standing,

Stephanie instantly responded to the leashed strength of him.

It was all too easy to imagine him, sabre in hand, at the head of a charging army of marauding Tartars! His arm lifted and involuntarily she drew back, startled. But he was only opening the door for her, and, feeling an idiot, she said goodbye to him and walked from his sleekly modern office—incomprehensibly modern considering his old-fashioned attitudes!—into the hot afternoon sunshine.

Her hotel was a few blocks away, and she made for it, oblivious of the teeming crowds pushing past her to get to the market stalls lining every inch of pavement.

She was still staggered by the strange contrast Mr Hamid presented. Granted, she had won this round, but she had a horrible suspicion it was a hollow victory, and he would be watching like a hawk for her to put a foot wrong—after which she would be unceremoniously dispatched to England, marked 'Unwanted—Too Fragile!'

She chuckled at the notion, her humour returning. This client might be tough, but so was she. When it came to her profession she was a match for anyone, and nobody, but nobody, was going to intimidate her!

Reaching Tamsin Square, she entered the lobby of the Hotel Marmara, five-star luxury and affording a marvellous view of the Black Sea. Yet the thought of staying in a hotel for the months she would be here did not appeal, and she determined to find an apartment.

She went over to Reception for her key, a lissom figure in blue, wafting *Femme*. Tall and curvaceously proportioned—playing down neither her height, which was above average, nor her firm, jutting breasts, which appeared larger because of her hand-span waist—she was used to being the focus of male eyes. Her mouth and nose, neat and pretty, commanded the least attention, this usually being caught by her almond-shaped eyes, an unusual blend of green and grey, one colour or other predominating, according to her mood. To this, add a silky mane of red-gold hair, loose and swinging, and it was easy to see why she was never short of admirers.

Aware of several now, she didn't know whether to have coffee down here or in her room. But the sun was shining and it seemed a pity not to take a dip in the pool.

Going to her room—why did it have to be so depressingly modern when it could as easily have been charmingly Turkish?—she changed into a black swimsuit, donned a towelling robe and went down to the garden.

The setting was breathtaking. Tropical foliage, splashed by brilliant-coloured flowers, surrounded a crystalline-blue pool sparkling high on a cliff top, seeming for all the world an extension of the vast expanse of sea beyond. Birds circled above her head, and an azure butterfly landed on a nearby hibiscus. Then a red-fezzed waiter came over to her, and the scene shivered into reality. Smiling at him, she ordered an iced coffee, at the same time dropping her things and herself on to a yellow sunbed under a matching umbrella.

Letting her Gucci sunglasses drop from atop her head to her nose, Stephanie gazed leisurely around her. She could have been in any luxury hotel favoured by the jet-set. Gorgeously tanned Mediterranean beauties and their generally older escorts lazed alongside the pool, and she resisted the urge to cover her creamy skin from the lascivious looks of men old enough to have fathered her!

Instead she finished her drink and, padding over to the water, dived into it. Like a sea nymph she surfaced at the other end, her mane of wet hair clinging to her head and shoulders, water sparkling jewel-like on her lashes. With smooth strokes she swam the length of the pool, then lifted herself on to its edge, eyes shut and face turned to the warmth of the sun.

Mr Hamid might try to make things difficult for her while she was here, but the never-ending sunshine in this land of many contrasts would keep her happy. On which admission she retrieved her bathing wrap and returned to her room to put through a call to John.

'I was waiting to hear from you.' His tone alerted her.

'Oh?'

'Very much "oh"! Mr Hamid was on the line half an hour ago.'

'Objecting to me, of course!'

'In italics!'

'Which leaves me where?'

'Firmly in Istanbul,' John Lister declared. 'I had a feeling it would get up his nose having to deal with a woman, but I didn't think he'd react quite so strongly. Anyway, I made it plain he'd have to choose between a man who knew nothing about the job, and a woman who did.'

'That must have given him food for thought!'

'He chomped on it for all of sixty seconds!' John chuckled. 'But he's a businessman first and foremost, and he realised it was in his interest to climb down.'

'Why do I have to apologise for being a woman?' Stephanie demanded angrily. 'The whole thing's infuriating.'

'I know. But forget it, and concentrate on our big fat fee!'

Try though she did, she was still seething at the Turk's arrogance an hour later as she stepped, poised and serene, from the elevator. No one would have guessed that the enchanting creature in shimmering blue silk harboured anything as ugly as resentment, least of all the black-haired, broad-chested man she almost bumped into as she rounded a marble pillar on her way to the dining-room.

What on earth was Tariq Hamid doing here?

'Good evening,' he said silkily. 'Reception couldn't get an answer from your room.'

'I must have been on my way down. Is it anything important?'

'Important enough to bring me here.'

He paused, and she wondered if she was supposed to get down on her knees in obeisance.

'I owe you an apology, Miss Rodgers,' he went on abruptly. 'I was unnecessarily rude to you this afternoon. You can't help being a woman any more than I can help being a man.'

'Big of you to realise it,' she said sarcastically. 'Only *I'm* not rude!'

'And hence have no need to apologise to me! I deeply regret my behaviour and hope you'll allow me to explain it to you over a drink.'

Not long ago Stephanie would gladly have poured one over his head, but, remembering the 'big fat fee' he represented, she nodded politely and walked beside him to the terrace.

At a table overlooking the moonlit sea, he ordered drinks—white wine for her, a whisky for himself—then began without preamble.

'I spoke to your senior partner after you left me this afternoon.'

'I know.'

He looked at her sharply. 'As I informed you earlier, I'm not used to having business dealings with women. Generally they're—er——'

'Your secretaries or servants?' she put in sweetly.

'Or contented and happy to leave the earning of money to the men in the family,' he said, ignoring her remark.

Stephanie swallowed hard. He couldn't be serious! But his expression showed he was and, swallowing any further sarcasm, she decided her best bet was to handle the situation like a sociologist who'd accidentally found a rare specimen for study.

'You obviously work in a different world from mine, Mr Hamid. In the West, women are treated as equals—personally as well as professionally.'

'And you're happy with such a situation?'

'I can't imagine any other.'

'A pity,' he said.

'You object to female equality?' Stephanie's control was beginning to slip.

'Depends what you mean by equality.'

'Mental capacity, Mr Hamid.'

'Women definitely aren't equal to men there! No, please, hear me out,' he ordered as she almost exploded. 'Women don't have the same capacity for logic, science, mathematics——'

'Rubbish!' Stephanie exploded.

'It isn't. How many great female composers are there? And what about painters, sculptors—chefs, even? As for science and philosophy, there are——'

'Do you mind if we change the subject?' Stephanie cut in again. 'Or I'll be the first British woman to be tried for murder in Turkey!'

He flung back his head and laughed, teeth gleaming white in his bronze-skinned face. All surliness gone, he was incredibly handsome. It's this damned moonlight and the shimmering Bosporus, she thought sourly, conscious of her trembling hand. Without question he was the Turkish answer to Adonis, but on the mental level they had as much in common as Gypsy Rose Lee and Mrs Pankhurst! It was incredible that a man of the world should hold such archaic views.

'My good intentions appear to have backfired on me,' his deep voice rumbled with amusement. 'I come here to apologise, and end up a prospective murder victim!'

'Maybe we should forget apologies, Mr Hamid, and stick to business.'

The broad chest lifted in an imperceptible shrug, drawing attention to his sleek silk jacket.

'Put it down to my Turkish upbringing,' he said, one finger of a long, slender hand rubbing the side of his cheek. 'I run my business the way my forefathers did—which means the leisurely discussion over endless cups of coffee, the genial ironing out of differences.'

'*I* didn't notice any "genial ironing out" in your attitude to me,' she retorted. 'It was more a flattening out!'

'Discovering you were a woman disconcerted me,' he admitted. 'My reaction was impolite, hence my coming here to make amends.' He paused, then went on, 'The Clinic is a memorial to my father and grandfather, and is therefore very dear to my heart, so I don't want its creation marred by any hostility between us.'

'I'm not in the least hostile towards you,' Stephanie lied.

'You surprise me.'

'A liberated woman takes dissenting males in her stride, Mr Hamid. She realises she's breaking new ground, and expects hostility.'

'How wearing on the nerves!'

'Not half as wearing as kowtowing to men who often have half one's ability!'

Black eyes narrowed. 'You are anti-men, Miss Rodgers?'

'I'm anti anyone who's obstinate and unreasonable.'

'I will try to be neither.'

'You mean you've had a change of heart?'

'Definitely not. But I'm taking John Lister's word that you're the best person to stand in for him.'

His glance ranged surreptitiously over her, though not

so surreptitiously that she wasn't conscious of it. Her hackles rose and it was great temptation not to give him the same insolent appraisal. But if she did, she would be asking for trouble.

'Having a beautiful woman in charge will have many advantages,' he added.

'Really?' Her voice dripped ice, and if he got the message he gave no sign of it.

'Yes, indeed. I can see all the contractors vying with each other for your approval.'

Stephanie seethed inside. The insolence of the man to infer she would resort to feminine wiles to get the work done! If only she dare let rip and say that even if she were plain as a pikestaff, the finished building would be a shining example of her company's expertise and talent! But the flag of diplomacy waved in front of her, and she swallowed her anger with the last of her wine.

'You flatter me, Mr Hamid.'

'You should be used to compliments.'

She shrugged and stood up. 'Could we forget the man and woman bit and continue as client and architect?'

'By all means.'

Diplomatically she gave him her hand. His grasp was bone-shattering, and it took every bit of her will-power not to wince. The gleam in his eye told her he had done it deliberately, as if to remind her that though they might talk man to man, physically he could bend her to his will.

Dropping some money on the table, he went with her to the lobby. 'Is your room comfortable here, Miss Rogers? I know the Manager and can have——'

'It's fine, thanks,' she said firmly. 'But, in any event, I intend moving. Hotels are so impersonal; I'd much rather be in an apartment.'

'Do you have one in mind?'

'No. I'm going to start hunting around tomorrow.'

'Mind which area you choose. Some aren't suitable for

women living alone.'

'I'm used to taking care of myself.'

'In your own country, maybe. But you're in the Middle East now, and would do well to remember it.'

'I will, Mr Hamid. Thank you.'

Of course, she had no intention of listening to him! He probably thought she should stay in some ghastly modern block in a new suburb with as much Turkish atmosphere as Clapham! Whereas what she had in mind was a place in the Old Town, where she could imbibe the sights and smells of Istanbul. Still, she appreciated his concern for her well-being, especially after having done his best to steamroller her into the ground!

'Then we are friends?' he asked, cutting into her thoughts.

'Yes, Mr Hamid,' she replied and, watching him saunter off, reluctantly conceded he would be an interesting man to know, but a dangerous one to know too well.

For her peace of mind, and the continuing prosperity of Lister and Young, she would do her darnedest to steer clear of him.

CHAPTER TWO

No city in the world went about its daily business with as much hustle and bustle as Istanbul, and a quarter to eight next morning saw Stephanie braving the chaotic commotion of the avenues that would take her to the Clinic.

She couldn't help contrasting the smartly dressed men and women of European Istanbul, thronging the pavements on their way to work, with the peasant women in pantaloons sitting in doorways peeling potatoes to the chant of music coming from the nearby bazaar—which was so crowded that from a distance it was impossible to discern any movement!

Resisting the urge to go and explore it, she turned into the avenue where the Hamid project was already rising from the ground, an avenue of shiny limousines depositing dignitaries at entrances to imposing, ornately fashioned buildings. How evident the rub of the old and the new in a few short blocks! And how ancient and magical the domes and minarets of Istanbul's famed Blue Mosque, visible through the misty sunlight.

Blending the Clinic into the surrounding architecture had been an interesting challenge for their company, requiring months of painstaking research before they had completed their designs and won the Turk's instant approval.

Stephanie quickened her step the nearer she drew to the sounds of building work, enjoying the raucous whirr of the pneumatic drill, the steady beat of the hammer, the clickety-clack of the concrete mixer. Labourers were already milling around, lugging heavy wheelbarrows and shinning up and down the scaffolding to the sixth and top floor. No skyscraper this, but then they had tried to keep to the Byzantine style of the city.

She glanced at her watch. She would have a chat with Mustafa, the Clerk of Works, then go to the builders' merchants to see the bathroom fittings he had found. On her last visit, he had tried to persuade her and John to take highly ornate ones, but had finally agreed to give them pastel colours. This was a clinic, after all, not a bordello!

Stepping carefully over the rubble, red-gold hair glinting in the sunshine like a newly minted coin, she went into the prefab office that stood where the car park was going to be, stopping in surprise as she saw Mr Hamid talking animatedly to Mustafa.

'Good morning, Miss Rodgers.' The dark head inclined in her direction. 'I won't be long.'

Hiding her curiosity, she waited, not understanding what they were saying, since her Turkish didn't go beyond the merest pleasantries, and seething with indignation that he didn't have the manners to speak English in front of her. As the client, he was entitled to come here whenever he wished, but at least he should have the decency to speak a language the three of them could understand, and not leave her hovering beside him like a dummy.

Impatiently she tapped her foot, and though his swift, downward glance told her he had seen it, he went on talking. He really was insufferable!

'If there's anything I can do to help . . .?' she put in, not giving a damn that she was cutting across him.

'No, thank you,' Tariq Hamid said smoothly.

Feeling as useless as a plug in a sieve, Stephanie regarded the leonine head, with its springing, shiny black hair, bent over the worksheet spread before him. If this visit presaged daily ones, she would end up strangling him! He might be allowing a woman architect to supervise his building, but he himself obviously intended supervising the architect!

'I'm finished.' He straightened and looked at her.

'If there's anything else you wish to know,' she said with forced calm, 'perhaps you'd ask *me*. I can come to your office each week, if you prefer.'

'There's no need for hard and fast rules, Miss Rodgers. I can drop by whenever I'm passing. Unless you think I don't trust you?'

'Would it matter if I did?'

'No.'

He certainly didn't mince words—that much could be said for him. With an effort, Stephanie swallowed hers. But oh! what temptation to tell him what she thought of him!

'As you know,' he went on, 'I've been abroad for most of this year so I couldn't watch the building grow, which I'd hoped to do. But I expect to be here till autumn, and will enjoy following its progress. I'm sorry if my presence will annoy you.'

How easily he had read her thoughts! In future she'd have to monitor them. 'On the contrary, Mr Hamid,' she said with veiled sarcasm, 'it's reassuring to have a strong, capable man behind me should anything go wrong.'

'I'm glad you think so.'

Their eyes met, and she saw no vestige of humour in his. Dear heavens, he'd taken her seriously!

'I was being sarcastic, Mr Hamid.'

'How regrettable.' With a nod to Mustafa, and a stiff bow in her direction, he left.

Without his overpowering presence, the little hut felt spacious, though it took a few moments for Stephanie's temper to subside sufficiently for her to concentrate on the business in hand.

In the six weeks since she and John had been here, the floors had been laid, as well as the conduits for the electricity and telephones. If things went on at this pace, the entire shell should be completed in a month.

'Mr Hamid is very knowledgeable man,' Mustafa remarked as he accompanied Stephanie around the site. He was a young Turkish Cypriot, and she and John found him able and likeable.

'Is he in property development?' she asked.

'He in many things. He very important man.'

'*He* thinks so, too,' she said drily, pretty sure that Mr Hamid had those long, strong fingers of his in many lucrative pies. If only he'd keep them out of this one!

It was late afternoon when she returned to the hotel and, retrieving her key, asked the Reception clerk if he could recommend an estate agent.

'I'll give you the name of the best,' he said, earnestly scribbling on a card. 'Shall I ask the operator to call them for you?'

'No, thanks. I'll do it from my room.'

The telephone was ringing as she opened her door and, amused by the man's enthusiasm, she hurried over to answer it. But the voice at the other end was English, not Turkish, and public school to boot.

'Miss Rodgers? James Edgar here. I'm a friend of John Lister's. He suggested I call and introduce myself. I'm with the Consulate, and if there's anything I can do . . .'

'How kind—but I'm fine, thanks. Unless you know of an apartment to rent?'

'You don't like the Marmara? I understood it was excellent.'

'It is, but hardly the sort of place to come home to from a dusty building site!'

'I take the point,' he chuckled. 'I'll have a word with some of my colleagues here. There's generally someone coming or going who'd be happy to do a short let. Maybe we can have dinner one evening, and you can give me a clearer idea of what you want.'

'I'd like that.'

'How about tonight—if you're free, that is?'

He was a fast worker, but with John's recommendation, she should be OK, thought Stephanie.

'Tonight's fine,' she answered. 'I've never been alone in Turkey before, and I was preparing myself for an attack of the blues!'

'Musicwise only, from now on!'

She laughed. 'How will I recognise you?'

'I'll recognise *you*. John's given me a detailed description.'

As Stephanie showered and changed, she thought how like John it was to get someone to befriend her, and hoped James Edgar was as nice as he sounded.

At first sight, he seemed to be. Neat-featured, tall, slim and blond, with cool blue eyes and a warm smile, he was standing by the elevator to greet her as she stepped from it.

'You must be Stephanie,' he stated. 'John wasn't exaggerating when he——'

'Nice meeting you, Mr Edgar,' she intervened.

'James, please, and it's even nicer meeting *you*.'

Here was a charmer if ever there was one—and top drawer, too: two attributes that didn't necessarily go together!

Like Professor Higgins in *My Fair Lady*, she made a mental assessment of him: public school without question, and university educated—not a red-brick one, either. Aristocratic background, she was sure, and possibly a title in the offing.

As guesses went, it was spot on, for over drinks at a restaurant near the harbour his conversation confirmed it. He didn't try the guessing game with her, however, for he openly plied her with questions.

'My parents are doctors, and my two brothers vets,' she said, satisfying his curiosity.

'A very caring family!'

'They thought me frightfully callous choosing architecture!'

'Why did you?'

'I love buildings. Old ones, especially.'

'Most architects *I* know prefer tearing 'em down and putting up new ones!'

'You don't move in the right circles.'

'I will, from now on!'

He was flirting with her and she responded, enjoying meeting a man who admired her for what she was.

'So you've taken over from John?' he remarked.

'Yes. And it won't be easy.'

'I should think you can do it with your eyes closed.'

'And trip over Tariq Hamid!'

'Ah!'

'That's a very diplomatic "ah".' She sipped her raki—a grape mash watered down and flavoured with aniseed. 'I take it you know him?'

'Yes, indeed.'

'Then perhaps you can tell me what makes him tick.'

'That's a pretty tall order.'

She waited, watching a variety of expressions flit across his face as he debated where to begin.

'Well, the man's a strange mix of the past and the present,' he said. 'Sophisticated and westernised on the surface, but a true die-hard underneath. In Tariq's case it has as much to do with his being a Turk as coming from a Muslim background.'

'So he's a Muslim? I'd wondered.'

'He isn't actually. He grew up in that atmosphere, and some of their attitudes have rubbed off on him.'

'Especially when it comes to women,' she said, so vehemently that James laughed.

'You've come up against it, then?'

'Several times.' Lightly she sketched in her meetings with the man. 'Quite honestly,' she concluded, 'I can't figure out where I stand with him. When I first met him, he was infuriatingly anti-feminist and rude. Yet when he came to the hotel he was charm itself.'

'Maybe he draws a line between social occasions and business ones. If you take my advice, you'll——' James stopped and shook his head. 'Sorry, I shouldn't interfere!'

'Oh, please, you're not. After all, you've lived here long enough to have some idea how these people tick, and if you can put me wise . . .'

James pulled a face. 'You'll probably hate me for saying this—and in England or the States I'd bite my tongue out before I did, but in the Middle East . . . What I mean is that you should take advantage of being a woman. Don't try fighting him on *his* terms, Stephanie. If you do, *you'll* be the one to end up flat on your face! You've much more chance of bowling him over with a smile, a whisper of silk, a waft of *Diorissimo*, and before you can say Kemal Atatürk, he'll be kneeling at your feet!'

'If he hasn't already chopped them down at the knees!'

'I'll back a red-gold blonde any day!'

She laughed, and nibbled on an olive. 'Fill me in a bit more on his background.'

'Business or personal?'

'Both.' She stifled her guilt to be gossiping like this. After all, they were English compatriots talking about a foreigner, so there was no reason to be coy!

'His grandfather founded the family fortune,' James began. 'Made it in carpets, and invested the proceeds in property abroad.'

'Very far-sighted!'

'Far enough to have his son—Tariq's father—spend his formative years in the States. But the minute the young man showed signs of taking an American wife, he hauled him back and married him off to a cousin.'

'Without objection?'

'In this country the father's wish is law, and family loyalty counts above everything.'

'Is the grandfather still alive?'

James shook his head and signalled for their wine to be replenished. 'He died last year—two years short of a century, and none of his faculties impaired. I met him twice and found him very impressive. Tariq takes after him.'

'And his father?'

'Died when Tariq was ten. So he was practically raised by the old man. He was sent to New York, too, and also spent some time in Paris at a merchant bank.'

'I shouldn't have thought that necessary,' Stephanie said drily. 'Turks have a reputation for being shrewd.'

'But add French finesse and American dynamism, and you've got yourself a formidable opponent!'

'How come you know so much about the Hamid family?' she asked.

'I play squash with one of Tariq's brothers-in-law.'

'I didn't realise he was married.'

'He isn't—it's his sister's husband. Tariq's unusual in that he's still single in his mid-thirties. Most Turks marry young, and his refusal to follow the pattern was a bone of contention between him and his grandfather. I gather a girl's been chosen for him, though.'

'She has my sympathy,' Stephanie sniffed.

'He's not as bad as that,' James grinned. 'Socially, he's extremely likeable. And you should try to wangle yourself an invitation to his home. As an architect, you'll find it intriguing. It's a veritable palace.'

'That figures for a man who acts like an emperor!'

James laughed outright. 'He's really got up your nose, hasn't he?'

'Silly of me,' she admitted. 'I don't usually let a client get to me like this. Must be something to do with living on the job and feeling foreign and alone.'

'Well, you're not alone any longer,' James murmured, and she gave him a warm smile, unexpectedly pleased to have met him.

For the rest of the evening their talk was general, James proving an amusing companion. A handsome one too, with his aquiline nose, dark eyebrows—unusual in someone so blond—and blue eyes that crinkled at the corners when he smiled. She had never been partial to fair men, but was beginning to think it was simply a childish prejudice.

'I'm giving a brunch party Saturday,' he announced as he signed the bill. 'I hope you'll come?'

'I'd like to. Where do you live?'

'Ten minutes from here. But it's best to take a taxi.'

Returning to her hotel at midnight, Stephanie was surprised to find a message from Tariq Hamid's secretary, giving her an address to go to for an apartment. She was intrigued that he had taken the trouble, though recollecting his warning that she be careful where she lived, decided he was being bossy rather than solicitous!

First thing next morning, armed with a street map, Stephanie made her way to a quiet side street not far from the hotel. Expecting an estate agents' office, she was puzzled to find a four-storey house. Still, many firms used houses these days, and she climbed the short flight of steps to the ornate front door and rang the bell.

'You must be Miss Rodgers,' greeted her almost instantly as the door was flung open by a tall, angular woman in her sixties, a brightly patterned cotton dress flowing around her. 'Tariq said you'd be calling,' she went on, her American accent evident. 'Where's your luggage?'

'My luggage?'

'There's no point wasting money on a hotel once you have your own place, is there?'

Stephanie stopped in her tracks. What on earth——! 'You *are* an estate agency, aren't you?'

'Hardly,' the woman laughed, lifting a hand to tuck wisps of curly greying hair into the bun from which it had straggled free. 'I'm May Constable and this is my home. Didn't Tariq tell you he'd taken an apartment for you here?'

Stephanie swallowed hard. 'I must have misread his message.'

'Well, come in and I'll show it to you.'

In silence Stephanie followed the woman to the second floor, vowing that even if the apartment was as luxurious as a Dynasty mansion, she'd still refuse to rent it! Who did that damn Turk think he was, taking for granted that he could choose where she should live?

Except she couldn't have chosen better herself. The three rooms she was shown were bright and welcoming; furnished in a mixture of early American and ancient Turkish, with mosaic-tiled floors scattered with brightly coloured kelims. Only the kitchenette and bathroom were modern, and the bed was a well-sprung double one.

'When will you move in?' Mrs Constable asked and, as Stephanie regarded her open, friendly face, she found it hard to fathom how such a likeable person could be a friend of her autocratic client.

'I—er—as soon as possible,' she heard herself say. 'Tomorrow?'

'Fine. Now, how about joining me for coffee?'

Relaxing on the comfortable davenport in the living-room of her future landlady's home, Stephanie felt delightfully at ease. The furnishing was the same as upstairs, except for a vast number of books, and many oil paintings, the most noticeable being a large portrait of a young May Constable.

'My husband loved this place,' the woman murmured, following Stephanie's gaze around the room. 'When he died three years ago, I couldn't bring myself to leave it, nor Turkey either for that matter. Not after living and working here for twenty years.'

Stephanie found herself warming to this woman with the flyaway hair and the many-changing expressions. She would be doing herself a favour to forget all pettiness and accept that Mr Know-All had found her an ideal place to live and an even more ideal landlady.

'What kind of work do you do?' she asked.

'I write thrillers.'

'My favourite reading! But I'm afraid I don't know your books.'

There was a slight hesitation. 'I—I use the name M.C. Andrews.'

Stephanie nearly dropped her cup. 'That's fantastic! I adore your books, especially the ones you set in the eighteenth century. They have the most marvellous atmosphere.'

'That was because of Joe—my husband. He was a historian and always enjoyed doing research for me.'

She fell silent, and Stephanie tactfully looked away.

'Before he died he made me promise not to stay here

alone.' Mrs Constable was in control of herself again. 'An Australian doctor lodged here for a year, then his sister took over the lease until a month ago. I was thinking about getting someone else when Tariq called me. How long do you think you'll be staying?'

'Three or four months.'

'If there's anything I can do to make your stay an enjoyable one . . .'

'Living in this house will be enough,' Stephanie said impulsively. 'It has such a lovely atmosphere . . . of joy and contentment.'

'I'm so glad you feel it. Not many people have such a quick reaction. But Joe and I were idyllically happy here, and I guess it's rubbed off on the walls!'

'I hope it rubs off on me,' Stephanie smiled and, downing her coffee, took her leave of May Constable until the following day.

CHAPTER THREE

STEPHANIE moved into the apartment early next morning—anxious to get settled before she was bogged down with work.

As expected, she felt instantly at home and, after unpacking and setting out some family photographs, she set off for the site. She half hoped Mr Hamid would show up today so she could thank him for finding her the apartment, and was disappointed when he didn't. Still, it would be easier thanking him over the telephone.

On her way home that afternoon, she stopped at the market to shop for food—finding it far more exciting to browse around the stalls than wheel a trolley along the aisles of a London supermarket. An hour later she returned home laden with bags of exotic fruit and vegetables, and some strange cuts of meat. She hadn't a clue how to cook some of it, and hoped May had a Turkish recipe book she could borrow!

Or she could always take lessons from James, Stephanie decided with amusement two days later, when she walked into his home and glimpsed the buffet table set with delectable-looking food.

Normally not a great one for parties—especially when all the guests were strangers to her—she found James an excellent host who introduced her to everyone, and was thoroughly enjoying herself, when a deep voice spoke behind her.

'Miss Rodgers?'

Cheeks red as her cotton shirtwaister, Stephanie swung round to see Tariq Hamid. In a flash she took in the sardonic smile, the raised black eyebrow, the cream linen suit and tie. A handsome, sensual man of power—and did he know it!

'I hadn't realised you knew James,' he commented, his eyes ranging over her.

'I was about to say that to you, Mr Hamid.' She gave him a frigid smile. 'I'd like to thank you for finding me the apartment.' She hoped she wasn't coming across as too enthusiastic. 'I called your office a few days ago but——'

'I was in Cairo,' he intervened smoothly. 'I'm glad you like it, though.'

Damn him! She hadn't said she did. 'An apartment's an apartment,' she shrugged, twirling the stem of her glass. She knew she was being less than polite but couldn't help it. Anyway, he was probably too conceited to notice.

'I thought you'd enjoy a view of the water,' he went on, 'and that you'd prefer living somewhere more redolent of Old Istanbul than a heartless modern block.'

Not quite as thick-skinned as she had imagined, she realised ruefully, and from the slight curl of his mouth knew he had again guessed what was going through her mind.

'Why do I get the feeling you're annoyed with me for having helped you?' he questioned. 'I knew what you wanted, and also that Mrs Constable was looking for someone like you. It was therefore simple for me to satisfy two people with one telephone call.'

The more he said, the more childish he made her seem. She hesitated, torn between a desire to answer him back or smile sweetly, and was saved from a decision when he changed the subject completely.

'I can see you haven't eaten yet. Come, we will go together.'

Before she could protest, he placed a hand beneath her elbow and guided her to the buffet. But his presence had ruined her appetite, and she stood stupidly staring at the table, her plate empty in her hand.

'Not hungry?' he asked.

'Of course she is,' James declared behind her, and Stephanie was so glad to see him, she was hard put not to fling herself into his arms.

She edged closer to him, allowing him to fill her plate, and not surprised at how quickly her appetite had returned. From the corner of her eye she saw Tariq Hamid move away, and couldn't restrain a sigh of relief.

'Like that, eh?' James said.

'Afraid so. Silly of me, isn't it?'

'Very. As I said the other night, you should charm to disarm!'

'He'd be immune!'

'Don't you believe it! He's a man, isn't he?'

Before she could answer, James settled her on a sofa and sat beside her.

'Red suits you. You should wear it often.'

'Yes, sir.' She wagged her fork at him. 'The food's smashing. Did you cook it?'

'With a little help from my friends! But don't eat too much,' he warned softly. 'I've planned to take you for a drive along the coast later this afternoon, and then have dinner in one of the fishing villages.'

'Sounds lovely.'

She looked forward to the prospect of spending a few hours with this most likeable man. She shifted in her chair to put Mr Hamid out of her line of vision, as well as her mind. She would be darned if she'd let him sour her afternoon!

It became a distinct possibility though, for as they were sipping their coffee James was called to the telephone, returning some moments later to say he would have to take a rain check for the rest of the day.

'Looks as though I'll be tied up at the Consulate till late tonight.'

'Never mind,' she said philosophically. 'I've a stack of work myself.'

'I wouldn't dream of letting you work on such a beautiful day.' Tariq Hamid had come up quietly beside them. 'Sorry to barge in on you like this, but I couldn't help overhearing. And since James has to put Queen and Country first, perhaps you'll allow me to stand in for him?'

'There's really no need for you to trouble,' Stephanie said quickly.

'It would be my pleasure.'

'No, honestly.'

'I think it's a great idea,' James interposed, giving Stephanie such a disarming smile she could cheerfully have strangled him. He knew darn well the Turk was the last man she wanted to spend any time with! Talk about the British sense of humour!

'Very well, Mr Hamid. I'll be—er—delighted to go with you.' She tried not to sound ungracious, but from the man's expression knew she hadn't succeeded.

What a joyride this was going to be! For the life of her she couldn't imagine what they would find to talk about. Business, probably; whether she thought costs would escalate; whether she was happy at the progress being made . . . Hardly an uplifting conversation for her day off! Still, she'd have to grin and make the best of it.

Less than an hour later, she found herself sitting beside her client in his silver-grey BMW, heading towards the Bosporus.

'It was nice of you to ask me out,' she said to his profile. 'I didn't expect it.'

'I find that surprising.'

'Why?'

'A beautiful woman like yourself should expect to be invited out.'

'I do,' she admitted frankly. 'But not by you.'

'Am I different from other men, then?'

His question reminded her of what James had said earlier, and a frisson of fear shivered through her. 'You're a client, Mr Hamid. That puts you into a different category.'

'Even clients are human, Miss Rodgers.' His voice was deep, the accent faint yet noticeable. 'And being human, I find you beautiful, amusing and interesting. I may disapprove of a woman doing a man's job, but I can still recognise her sex appeal.'

Good God! She almost asked him to stop the car so she could get out and stalk off. Only the fear of being stranded in the middle of nowhere prevented her and, stony-faced, she stared through the windscreen.

'I've annoyed you again, haven't I?' he said.

'I'm used to that from you, Mr Hamid. In fact, not to cut too fine a point, I find you exceedingly difficult.' The instant she spoke, Stephanie regretted her frankness, for he favoured her with a glacial stare.

'You will explain yourself, please.'

Stephanie winced. If only she hadn't accepted his damned invitation! She had no idea if she could control her dislike of him, yet knew that if she didn't, she might well be on the next plane home—and John would have her hide!

'Don't censor your answer, Miss Rodgers. I want you to be truthful.'

'So you can chuck me off the job?' she asked with what she hoped was the right amount of amusement.

'You think I'd use a private conversation between us to do that?'

'I——'

'Enough! Clearly you do.'

He lapsed into brooding silence, and after a moment she said awkwardly, 'I'm sorry, Mr Hamid. I didn't mean to offend you.'

'You haven't. I'm just disturbed that my behaviour has led you to think I could be unethical. But to get back to my original question. Why do you find me difficult?'

Accepting that evasion was out, Stephanie drew a deep breath. 'Because of the way you behave over the Clinic. You come to see how the work's progressing nearly every day—which I gather you never used to do, and——'

'You object to that?' he intervened silkily.

'Of course not! I merely object to you ignoring me. And quite honestly, there must be a better way of checking up on me.'

'Is that what you think I'm doing?'

He was so astonished that he turned his head to look at her, narrowly missing running over a chicken that had escaped from a crate being unloaded by the roadside. Muttering in Turkish, he steadied the car.

'I visit the site because I enjoy seeing the building grow. You already know it means a great deal to me. As for my ignoring you when I'm there . . . I do so simply because I don't want you to think I'm interfering.'

'And checking up with Mustafa *isn't* interfering?' she asked tightly.

'He merely explains what's going on; technical details I'm reluctant to bother you with.'

'I'm happy to explain anything you want to know. I've already told you.'

'Thank you.' The dark head inclined. 'But no man

enjoys showing his ignorance.'

Especially to a woman! she thought, but aloud said, 'Even the most brilliant man doesn't know everything.'

She was by no means sure she accepted his explanation, but gave him full marks for coming up with it! At least it proved he didn't want open warfare, though she was still convinced he felt no woman architect was capable of supervising anything more technical than a sandcastle!

Her temper remained at simmering level, but gradually the beauty of the scenery made her cool down. They were travelling over the suspension bridge linking Europe and Asia; below them lay the gleaming waters of the Bosporus—the narrow waterway dividing it—and, wide-eyed, she took in the magnificent panorama stretching around her: the myriad minarets and spires of Istanbul piercing the bright blue sky, the pastel-coloured fishing villages strung along the coastline and basking in the golden glow of the afternoon.

Only when they had left the bridge behind them did Tariq Hamid draw the car to a stop and break the silence.

'I gather James was going to take you to one of our fishing villages,' he said, 'but I can offer you a choice. Either that, or a boat ride to the Islands. A ferry leaves every hour.'

Surprised, Stephanie turned to face him. Not only did he sound different—his tone light and easy—but he looked it, too; the firm mouth softened by the faintest of smiles, the lines either side of it lessened by his relaxed expression, showing her a side to him she guessed he reserved for women in his own circle—a handsome, sensual man of power.

'I rather fancy the Islands,' she replied stiltedly.

'I'm glad we agree on something!' Switching on the

ignition, he made for the landing wharf, and soon they were parked and boarding the ferry.

It was already chock-a-block with passengers: tourists with cameras and guide books, peasants in the inevitable black, with their usual assortment of bundles, children and livestock.

'We'll get off at Büyükada,' her escort stated. 'It's the largest and most picturesque of the Princes' Islands.'

'Tell me about them,' she said, keen to steer the conversation away from the personal.

'Well, they were originally called Priests' Islands—because of the dozens of monasteries the Greek Orthodox church built on them. But when the Byzantine princes started using the islands as a playground, the name was changed. Today, of course, they're holiday resorts for everyone.'

The breeze ruffling the waters lifted Stephanie's hair, and she breathed in the fresh salt air, thinking how much more she would have enjoyed this trip with James beside her. She had never before felt at such a disadvantage with anyone, and wondered what there was about Tariq Hamid that set her nerve-ends jangling. Was it only because his views on career women had ruffled her feathers too much for her to smooth them down?

Whatever the reason, it was foolish to let him affect her. She would be here for at least another three months, and unless there was some form of *modus vivendi* between them, it would be very wearing. Perhaps if this outing passed peacefully, they might end up friends. Or if that was too much to hope for, then respected business acquaintances.

If the man had any idea what was passing through her mind, he gave no sign of it and, with the ease of someone who knew the scene well, pointed out the sights as the Islands came closer. Monasteries and convents were to the fore, some in use, but most in ruins.

'For many years, sultans used them to imprison relatives they didn't see eye to eye with,' he explained.

'With the size of harems I should imagine a few mothers-in-law were included!' Stephanie couldn't help saying, and had the surprise of hearing him laugh, a full-bodied sound that rumbled through his chest, making her conscious of its breadth and strength.

Funny, but she had never associated Turks with being physically overpowering, imagining them more wiry. But this man had the physique of an American baseball player. Not quite as exaggerated perhaps, but well over six foot with a build to match.

Even as she eyed him, he shrugged off his jacket against the heat of the day. His cream silk shirt emphasised his swarthiness, and the thick ripple of muscles across his shoulders. The breeze lifting her hair caught the silky jet strands of his, though not even the breeze dared do more than lightly ruffle it.

'Why are you smiling?'

She hadn't known she was until his question, and because it took her unawares, answered truthfully. 'I was thinking even a breeze daren't ruffle you!'

He chuckled deeply. 'Only *you* dare, Miss Rodgers.'

'Would you rather I was afraid of you?'

'Would I rather a kitten had no claws? Remove them, and it's defenceless.'

Irritated by his method of cutting her down to size, she spoke sharply. 'I know I annoy you by not conforming to your outmoded concept of how a woman should behave, but I come from a different culture, Mr Hamid, as I keep reminding you.'

Their eyes locked, and with a shock she saw his weren't black, as she had supposed, but a warm dark brown.

'You're right,' he said slowly, resting his arms on the rail. 'It's foolish of me not to remember you come from the West, with a life-style that the women in *my* life would regard as alien.'

'Sounds as if you inhabit a very rarefied world,' she muttered. 'The girls *I've* seen in Istanbul could as easily be at home in London or New York!'

'A country shouldn't be judged by its capital. Travel the countryside and you'll meet women who are happy to live as their mothers and grandmothers did.'

'And they're the ones you admire?' she asked incredulously.

'They are happy,' he asserted. 'What is there not to admire?'

'They might be even happier if they had a chance to express themselves!'

'They do that by caring for their men, their children and their homes. Female liberation has brought more problems than benefits.'

'Problems for men,' Stephanie snorted. 'They have to get used to managing without willing slaves!'

'An emancipated woman can also be a slave. Trying to combine a job with running a home, caring for children . . . She has to be working woman, wife and mother.'

'With a husband who shares the chores,' Stephanie added, and saw his mouth lift in wry amusement.

'Do you really believe that? A couple may start out with the intention of share and share alike, but it's still the woman who bears the children, and it's her career that inevitably suffers.'

'Most firms give maternity leave.'

'Which frequently furthers someone else's ambition. Step off the corporation ladder—for whatever reason—and another person's waiting to take your place.' He paused. 'No argument, Miss Rodgers?'

'Not when you're right. And in this instance you are. But that's only because men are still calling the shots. Once there are more women at the top, things will change. It also takes a while to re-educate men's thinking. But that will happen too, eventually.'

'How do you re-educate *feelings*?' Tariq Hamid asked suavely. 'Not only men's but women's? Many working wives are torn between their careers and family and, if their children should be ill and need them, they're stretched on an emotional rack.'

'I'm not saying it isn't a problem,' Stephanie admitted. 'But the Women's Movement is a pioneer one, and pioneers generally suffer in the beginning.'

'None of the women *I* know suffer,' came the instant reply. 'They are contented wives and mothers.'

'What would you have done if your sisters had wanted to follow a profession?'

'Tried to dissuade them.'

'By locking them in their rooms and putting them on a bread and water diet?'

'*Gentle* persuasion. It gets better results—always.'

Pink-cheeked, she met his eyes, and noting the twinkle in them, breathed more easily.

'Let's not go on discussing female emancipation,' she suggested. 'Our ideas are so opposed, we're bound to come to blows.'

'I'd never hit the weaker sex!'

His deep voice was even deeper with amusement, its reverberation making her conscious of his well muscled chest. Despite his veneer of sophistication, she knew that if one removed the stylish clothes and the layer of Western education, there would be little difference between him and his autocratic grandfather.

Turning to face the sea, she saw the ferry was approaching Büyükada, giving her a clear view of the pine-forested hills, lush valleys, olive groves and vineyards. Tariq Hamid hadn't exaggerated when he had said it was a beautiful island.

Her eyes went from the seagulls swooping through the sunlit sky to the harbour filled with boats, most of them small and brightly coloured, then to the villas perched on the hills like so many pastel fruit-drops, surrounded by luxuriant gardens.

'What gorgeous flowers! Now I know what's missing in Istanbul. There are hardly any flowers or window-boxes.'

The man beside her shrugged off the criticism. 'Breathe the air. It's the purest in Turkey.'

Stephanie did as ordered. It certainly was. She inhaled another lungful and eyed the sunbathers sprawled on the shining white sands.

'You can see why it's such a popular place,' Tariq Hamid went on, taking her arm as the ferry docked, and leading her to a wickerwork ponycart.

Stephanie climbed up and blissfully sank into the cushioned seat, glad of the gaily striped awning, shading her from the blazing sun.

'I thought we'd take a ride around the Island, if that's all right with you?'

'You're the boss.'

He took his place beside her. 'You wouldn't care to put that in writing?'

'Definitely not!'

With a click of his fingers to the driver, and a swift command in his own tongue, they set off on their tour.

Ever after, Stephanie was to remember her afternoon on the island as an idyllic interlude.

Tariq Hamid was marvellously knowledgeable, regaling her with snippets of Turkish history and customs, using his charm to persuade the caretaker of a vacant summer-house—nestling in the hills overlooking the sea—to show them over it; introducing her to the dark, squat owner of an olive grove, who shared with them a bottle of rough red wine and black olives steeped in brine.

She had a feeling of going back in time, partly because of the island's setting, and partly the absence of cars. It reminded her of a brief visit she had paid to Sark, and she found herself wishing she had been born into an earlier era, when the pace was leisurely and competition less fierce.

'You're very deep in thought,' her companion commented as their buggy brought them back to the square in the little seaside town that was the centre of Büyükada's life, with its sandy beaches, family hotels and bustling cafés.

'I was thinking how much the twentieth century's lost compared with what it's gained,' she confessed.

'Are we in debit or credit?'

'Debit, I'm afraid.'

'Indeed? I thought you'd be an advocate of the present.'

'I don't discount all of it! But in some respects I think we've thrown out the baby with the bath water.'

'The baby with the ...?' Black eyebrows drew together. 'You've lost me there, I'm afraid.'

'It means throwing away the good with the bad.'

'Ah, then we're in agreement.'

'Only on some things.'

His mouth thinned, and she wished she had held her tongue. But this magical isle was making her say things she shouldn't.

They reached a bustling street café, and with a swift movement Tariq stepped neatly ahead of a jean-clad young couple and commandeered the only vacant table. Stephanie slid into her seat, turning it slightly to enjoy the last rays of the setting sun, then glanced at her companion.

The golden light softened the hard planes of his face, finding curves she had never suspected. He was completely unaware of the impression he made, or that people around him felt the power he emanated, and responded to it accordingly—the jean-clad young couple by smilingly backing away from the table they had considered theirs, the waiter by instantly scurrying across to hand them a menu.

'I hope you're hungry?' the deep voice questioned.

'Absolutely not. That brunch of James's was awfully filling. But I'm happy to watch *you* eat,' she added with a smile.

'At least join me in a little something. I'm sure I can tempt you.'

Damn right he could, but not the way he meant! She stopped her errant thoughts. The sun wasn't hot enough for sunstroke, so what was the matter with her? One thing was certain. He was the most charismatic man she had ever met.

With a start she realised he was reading from the menu, and she forced herself to concentrate.

'. . . *hansi tavasi*—that's fried anchovies—and you'll never taste better; or there's *kadin budu*, which actually means "woman's thigh" but refers to meatballs with rice; and then there's——' He stopped, grinning as he saw her expression. 'I'm not making this up, I promise you. Ask James.'

'I'll take your word. But you can stop reading, thanks. I'll have what those people over there are having.'

He turned his head to look. 'Pancakes stuffed with ewe cheese.'

'Is there a euphemism for them?' she asked, straight-faced.

'Yes, indeed. But I don't want to embarrass you! Your cheeks are already an interesting pink.'

'I don't embarrass easily, Mr Hamid, but you're rather an intimidating man.'

'Is that why you don't call me Tariq?'

'You don't call me Stephanie,' she came back at him.

'Then we must both change—Stephanie.'

The shadow of a young waiter, a boy of about twelve, fell across their table, preventing Tariq from going on, for which she was devoutly grateful.

She watched him give their order, his tone mellifluous as he spoke his own language. And how warmly he smiled at the boy, his features softening as she had never imagined they could! Amazing that he wasn't married with children. In his society it was unusual to be single at his age. Curiosity pricked, though she knew she dared not satisfy it.

By the time they returned to the harbour to take the ferry to the mainland, the sky had darkened to purple. It was cooler too, and Tariq slipped on his jacket, instantly reverting to the contained man she knew.

Yet did she know him? Hardly at all. Although he had chatted freely today, it had been on subjects well aired, and his innermost thoughts were still hidden.

'You're wearing your contemplative look again,' he said into the silence. '"Penny for them", as they say in your country.'

'They're not worth anything.'

'Your thoughts are always worth something, Stephanie.'

She liked the sound of her name on his lips. 'I was thinking how much I've enjoyed this afternoon.'

'Me, too. We must repeat it.'

Repeat what? she wondered. The sightseeing, or each other's company? Either way it wasn't important. What mattered was that they had called a truce.

Stars were puncturing the dark sky like children's helium balloons when they reached the mainland and their car. As they headed towards Istanbul, Stephanie gasped at the view from the bridge, breathtaking with the shimmering lights of the city merging with the star-studded sky.

'Wonderful, isn't it?' Tariq agreed, hearing her blissful sigh.

'Incredible.'

She said nothing further, content to study the scene, then closed her eyes and tried to absorb it into her memory.

The sudden silence made her open them, and she saw they were parked on a headland overlooking the sea.

'I can't take in anything else,' she protested. 'I've had enough for one day.'

'*I* haven't,' he murmured, his arm coming across the back of her seat.

Before she knew it, his mouth came down on hers. Though his movement had been sudden and forceful, the kiss itself was gentle, his tongue lightly skimming her lips, his hand softly roaming her spine. Desire tingled through her and she relaxed against him, her mouth slightly parting. What was this kiss, after all? Nothing more than a pleasant end to a pleasant day.

Her fingers moved over his head, and she was amazed that his hair, so thick and vibrant, should be soft as silk to the touch; and more amazed still when he gave a husky exclamation and pressed his mouth to her eyelids, her temple, and down the side of her face to the tender hollow of her neck.

Nor did he stop there—his tongue, moist and warm,

was hungrily seeking the curve of her breasts swelling over the low neckline of her dress. At its touch, an uncontrollable spasm shivered through her, trembling her limbs and sending a shaft of desire—almost tangible—across the soft downy mound between her thighs.

Aware of it, he groaned deep in his throat, his hand roaming her back for the zip of her dress and swiftly lowering it.

'Tariq, no!'

Ignoring her cry, he burrowed his head lower to search out her hardening nipples.

Damn him! This was going too far. A light-hearted goodnight kiss was one thing, the intimacy he was now seeking quite another, and she pushed sharply at his chest. He took no notice, his hold on her tightening, his tongue continuing its pursuasive path down to the rosy buds.

'Tariq, stop it!'

Again he ignored her plea, and she was suddenly petrified. She tried to kick out, but the weight of his body prevented her, and instead she pummelled at his head. With an exclamation he fell back, and she wrenched free and reached for the door, intent on escape.

But as her hand found the handle, he lunged forward and caught her arm, pulling her hard round to face him. Wildly she tried to claw at his face but he was too strong for her, catching both her hands in fingers of steel.

'Stop it, Stephanie! You're not leaving the car. We're miles from anywhere and you've nowhere to run.'

This was a Tariq she had never seen before. Everything she had read about Tartars flooded her mind, and she sobbed with fear and rage.

'How dare you! I'll never let you . . . If you try I'll——'

'For God's sake!' he exploded. 'Is that what you think?

I only wished to kiss you! Nothing more.'

Pushing her away from him, he slid further back into his seat and clenched his hands round the wheel, his knuckles gleaming white in the dashboard glow.

'I can't believe you seriously thought I'd . . .' He shook his head. 'The last thing I wanted was to frighten you. I only wanted to hold you, touch you.'

His apology—disjointed, abject—dissolved her panic, and she was left feeling stupid for over-reacting to a situation most girls her age would have taken in their stride; as *she* would have done had it been any other man at any other time. But with this one she was like a nervous schoolgirl and had behaved accordingly.

'Forgive me,' he whispered.

She drew a deep breath. 'You're forgiven.'

'And it's forgotten too, I hope?'

'Of course,' she lied, knowing she wouldn't forget, and pretty sure he wouldn't, either.

In this, unpredictable man that he was, Tariq proved her wrong.

Next day he came into Stephanie's office as she was going through some plans with the electrical contractor, and behaved as if their day on Büyükada had never occurred, and his passionate embrace in the car was only a figment of her imagination!

Hell's bells! she thought furiously. If that's how he wants to play it, let him. She couldn't care less! Yet she did, very much. Because it demeaned her womanhood.

She did her best to steer clear of him in the following weeks but, almost as if to aggravate her, he visited the site daily, occasionally bringing one or another of his family: his two sisters—one thin, one plump—and both exquisitely dressed; his brothers, shorter versions of himself; and a plethora of dark-suited, heavy-featured men whom she took to be relatives or friends.

She started dating James more often, and as their friendship developed, so did her liking for him. They had many interests in common—music, the arts, politics, country . . . Ah, country! That was the strongest bond of all, and if she had any sense she would remember it. Unfortunately, memory of a broad-shouldered, black-haired Turk persisted.

She was not helped in forgetting him by his frequently figuring in James's and May's conversation; James, because Tariq—though not a politician—moved in the highest political circles, and May, because he had been a friend of her husband and, as such, kept him alive for her.

'The thing I find most intriguing about him,' May said one evening as they sat by the window, the overhead fan whirring softly behind them, a faint breeze drifting in from outside, 'is that though he's dynamic in business, he's a traditionalist where his family's concerned. The true patriarch. He arranged his sisters' marriages, and chose the brides for his twin brothers. They were fathers before they were twenty-three! Now I hear he's marrying off his youngest brother.'

'He doesn't practise what he preaches,' Stephanie said lightly. 'Though I gather there's a girl lined up for him.'

'You mean Lala Erim? Yes, a cute little thing. A friend of one of his nieces. But he hasn't committed himself yet.'

'Perhaps he wants to marry for love!'

'I doubt if he's ever thought about it,' May grinned, pushing some stray ends of hair back into the bun atop her head. 'A few months ago I read an article on marriage by someone who'd recently conducted a poll at Tokyo University, and you'll never believe their findings. More than three-quarters of the students said they'd be perfectly happy marrying the person of their parents' choice! Can you credit it? Maybe it's we Westerners who've got it wrong. Our divorce rate rather bears it out.'

'I'd still plump for free choice—and run the risk of it failing.'

'Me too.' May's pointed nose twitched with amusement. 'My parents had a bishop's son picked out for me, so Joe and I eloped!'

Laughter brought the conversation to an end, and shortly afterwards Stephanie went to bed. However, sleep eluded her, and all sorts of people drifted in and out of her mind—James, Tariq, and Freddy, the boyfriend her parents had never liked.

Funny, she hadn't thought of him in years; not since he'd come back from Canada and she had realised how their interests had diverged, and what a lucky break she'd had not marrying him. Yet if he hadn't accepted an assignment in Montreal, she might well have done—and lived to regret it. So maybe there was something to be said for arranged marriages, for letting logic rather than love, choose your partner.

She smiled in the darkness. Good thing her high and mighty client couldn't read her mind this time! Not that she was serious about it. Japanese poll or not, she still felt love—not expediency—should be one's yardstick when it came to marriage.

CHAPTER FOUR

THREE weeks later, Tariq gave a party to celebrate his younger brother's engagement, and to Stephanie's surprise she received an invitation.

By return she sent it back marked 'unable to attend', and was astounded when, the very next morning, he stormed into her office and slammed the white and gold card down on the desk in front of her.

'Why?' he demanded harshly. 'Is it because of what happened the night we came back from the Islands? You still think I meant you harm? Haven't you accepted my apology?'

She pressed back hard in her chair to stop her body shaking. 'It's—it's got nothing to do with that.'

'Then why won't you come?'

How to find a logical reason when she didn't have one? In the cold light of day, with his snapping glance enveloping her, the emotions he normally aroused in her seemed nonsensical.

'I—er—well, the party's a private one, and I think I'd feel out of place among your family and friends. I've never met them and——'

'You always disappear when I bring them here!'

'I'm always busy,' she lied.

'Which is why this party will be an excellent opportunity of introducing them to you,' he responded instantly. 'You are responsible for erecting a memorial to my father, and my family are looking forward to meeting you.'

So that was why he had asked her!

'Since you put it like that,' she murmured, 'I'll come.'

Without another word he stalked out, and it was a long while before she was able to pick up her pen and resume work.

Determined to look her best, Stephanie went shopping for a dress. The bazaar was fine for caftans and casual cottons, but the outfit she had in mind would only be found in one of the expensive boutiques on Cumhuriyet Cadessi, Istanbul's most exclusive shopping street.

She was not disappointed. Hardly had she strolled ten yards down its crowded length when a jewel of a boutique caught her eye. There was only one garment in its window, and she knew instantly it was the one for her!

The elegant woman who came forward to serve her evidently felt it too, for, learning Stephanie wanted a dress for an occasion, she removed the one from the window and carried it reverently into the changing-room.

Slipping it on, Stephanie stared at herself entranced. She was embraced in a shaft of sunlight, caught in the golden radiance that shimmered within the silken folds. The wisp of camisole top—a thousand sparkling bugle beads—reflected the buttercup-gold, dawn-pink and peach bloom of the sunray-pleated skirt that swirled around her as she moved before the mirror, transported into that special feminine heaven only entered by those lucky enough to be dressed by a master hand.

She was Princess Aurora come to life; Sleeping Beauty waiting to be awakened by a kiss. Who cared that it was wildly, madly extravagant? It was a dress for a dream; a dress to entice her prince.

'You look wonderful in it!' the woman exclaimed.

'I'll take it,' Stephanie said, needing no sales talk.

'Of course,' came the reply, as if the woman had considered it a foregone conclusion. 'There are shoes and bag to match,' she added, bringing out high-heeled sandals in which to dance away the night, and a tiny, beaded bag to hold the key when midnight struck and the princess had to return to her castle.

Walking from the boutique, lost in her dream, Stephanie knew quite clearly that James, charming though he was, could never be her prince. Between them lay no special tenderness, no breathless joy, no throb of passion to be shared. He was a friend and could never be anything else.

She sighed, wondering if there would come a time when, as in the Rodgers and Hammerstein song, she would look across a crowded room on 'some enchanted evening' and glimpse her future love. Until now, the crowded rooms had been smoke-filled, her future nothing other than a burgeoning portfolio of work.

But a career wasn't likely to satisfy her for ever. She wanted to share her life with a man who would appreciate that her need of a husband, children and home went hand in hand with her longing to create the beautiful buildings that filled her imagination. And that precluded men like Tariq Hamid—of whom there were far too many!

The thought of him was like chapped fingers rubbing on silk! The sooner the Clinic was finished and she left Turkey, the better. It would be a wrench leaving Istanbul, for the city was a delight to the eye, with its play of sunrises and sunsets on the Bosporus—the swirl of water that divided Asia from Europe, the past from the present.

Dressing for the party on Saturday night, Stephanie found herself increasingly curious to see Tariq's home. 'A palace', according to James, for the rich—despite Turkey being an egalitarian society—lived in splendour.

Imagination, even of the wildest kind, did not prepare her for the marble edifice of soaring arches and domes, rising like an Arthurian legend from the watery edge of the Bosporus, turning the carpet of purple water into a mirror image of its own glorious, glittering self.

A thousand lights sparkled from its windows, glinting like fireflies through the tall, dark cypresses guarding the lower floor from prying eyes. A palace, James had said? This was a home for the heavenly hosts!

'Quite something, isn't it?' With typical British understatement, James's cool, cultured tones brought her to earth with a bump.

'It certainly is,' she concurred, wryly conceding that it took an Englishman to cut a fantasy down to size!

The white and gold hall, its hexagonal ceiling shimmering with blue and green mosaics, was equally breathtaking. So, too, were the vast reception-rooms ablaze with crystal chandeliers, ivory silk at the windows, cream and gold velvet chairs and sofas ranging marble floors. Turkish rugs enveloped the foot, and the eye was caught by intricately carved tables displaying exquisite bibelots—mother-of-pearl boxes, tiny jade figurines, painted miniatures on ivory—while delicately glazed walls were festooned with priceless Islamic wall hangings, the whole scene indicative of Tariq's culture.

Stephanie was no stranger to luxury, her profession having taken her to many opulent homes, but she had seen none as lovely as this.

Strangely enough, it wasn't ostentatious. Everything fitted perfectly into the wondrous setting, making a magnificent backdrop for the bejewelled women and their escorts, their perfume and cigar smoke mingling with the subtle scent of incense.

Their low tones—in a variety of accents—melded with the music, and were interspersed by the soft explosion of champagne corks as golden liquid was poured into cut-glass goblets, silver spoons scraped caviar from Limoges plates, jewel-handled knives clinked on silver salvers of smoked salmon and *foie gras*.

All this Stephanie took in within one startled moment,

then her eyes swiftly roamed the room for her host.

She spotted him at once, towering easily above everyone, black hair gleaming, bronze skin glowing, mouth faintly smiling as he moved amiably from group to group. A faultless white dinner-jacket drew attention to broad shoulders, and tailored black trousers to long, powerful legs that brought him with surprising swiftness to her and James's side, as he saw her.

How many guises he adopted! The autocratic businessman, impeccable in tailored suit; the relaxed companion, tieless, with windblown hair; and now the smiling host, urbane in evening clothes. Yet none of these images added up to the whole man, for she knew the essence of him remained unrevealed, shown to a few members of his family, perhaps, but never to the outside world.

'Good to see you both.'

His greeting was punctilious even as his eyes told Stephanie she was beautiful—as James already had—and she hastily averted her head and accepted a glass of champagne from a waiter.

'I think you know quite a few people here,' Tariq said to James. 'Be a good chap and introduce Stephanie around.'

Typical, she decided crossly. The lord commands and his lackeys obey! But she mustn't be bitchy. As host, he was expected to talk to all his guests—no mean task in a gathering as large as this—and one which would leave him little opportunity to introduce a newcomer.

Still, she was glad to have James beside her instead of Tariq. It was bad enough having him a thorn in her side at work, without having him there socially, too!

James knew more of the guests than Stephanie had realised, though thinking about it she wasn't surprised, for the rich and famous liked courting diplomats, particularly young and eligible ones, a fact brought home to her by the subtly flirtatious glances many women cast him.

And what lovely women they were! The kind Tariq admired, she knew instinctively. Exquisitely dressed, perfectly at ease as they talked and sparkled with the best of their men! Yet, despite their sophistication, they had a sheltered air, as if the cold wind of reality hadn't touched their delicate olive skin, nor their lustrous dark eyes seen anything ugly, hungry or poor.

'How the rich live,' Stephanie murmured as she and James strolled over to the window.

'Naughty, naughty,' he chided. 'You shouldn't judge a book by its wrapping. That languid brunette with the almond eyes for example, is a pediatrician, and the one in red, with rubies to match, runs a left-wing magazine!'

'You're kidding! And Tariq invites her here?'

'He's a liberal!'

'Pull the other one!'

'No, seriously. He might balk at the women in *his* family working, but he's intelligent enough to appreciate he's battling against the tide.'

'Then why doesn't he give in?'

'He will—once the tide becomes a tidal wave!'

'Do you feel the same as he does?' Stephanie questioned.

'Let's not particularise,' James answered, so quickly that she laughed.

'You're not a man,' she teased, 'you're a chicken!'

'On the contrary. I'm a clever cockerel who knows when not to crow!'

She was still smiling at this when, half turning, her eyes fell on a middle-aged woman holding court on a gilt-framed settee. Black hair, frosted with grey, sprang back from a high forehead marked by thick eyebrows above narrow, dark eyes. Her black dress, high-necked and long-sleeved, was a perfect foil for a suite of diamonds

Queen Elizabeth would have delighted to wear, and Stephanie knew this was Mrs Hamid, for her son had the same cut to his jaw, and regal bearing. Though in his case it was better described as *over*bearing!

A stir interrupted her musing, and she saw double doors at the far end of the salon being opened, an indication that dinner was served.

Seated at one of the dozen circular tables in a room that echoed the splendour of the rest of the house, Stephanie found that her dinner companions were all Turkish, though if conversation and attitudes were anything to go by, they could easily have come from the West.

One couple worked in the family business, another were professionals—he an accountant, she a lawyer—while the third were doctors running a group practice in a northern suburb.

'Do you have many male patients?' Stephanie asked the woman.

'Now yes, but not for the first few years. There's still resistance of course, but it's like that in your country, too. And it doesn't only apply to doctors.'

'How true,' Stephanie admitted. 'We've hardly any women bank managers, and I can count our female judges on the fingers of one hand.'

'In Turkey I don't even need a hand for that,' the woman laughed, the rest of what she was going to say cut short by the arrival of the first course.

Though no stranger to Turkish delicacies, Stephanie found the meal a revelation not only to the palate, but the eye.

Bowls of yogurt and dill, spiced purée of lentils, and marinaded mushrooms were accompaniments to hors-d'oeuvres of assorted dolma. The palate was then cooled by pomegranate soup, pink in colour and delicate on the tongue. It brought a murmur of appreciation from the *cognoscenti*, for the fruit wasn't in season until October, and there was much speculation as to where it had been imported from.

The main course was baby lamb; crisp outside, pink within, served with golden barley and lemon-flavoured lima beans, after which the meal was rounded off by melons and peaches and bite-sized baklava, the pastry so light that only its almond filling prevented it from floating away!

'I've gorged enough to last me a week,' Stephanie sighed to James. 'Do the Hamids always eat like this?'

'I shouldn't think so for a minute. When I dined here with Tariq last month, we had steak and salad!'

Involuntarily her eyes swivelled to his table some distance away. He was deep in conversation with an extremely pretty, doll-like girl on his right and, though curious to know who she was, she would rather have lost her eye-teeth than asked.

'Lovely, isn't she?' James commented, following her gaze.

Still refusing to admit to interest, Stephanie countered with, 'Who are the others at his table?'

'His mother, his older sister and husband, the engaged couple and her parents, and Mr and Mrs Erim and their daughter Lala—she's the little brunette I just pointed out to you, and the one they've lined up for our illustrious host.'

'Looks like she's stepped from the cradle.'

James grinned. 'They say she was still in it when her mother and Tariq's hatched wedding plans!'

Stephanie studied her. Pretty, if you liked sultry, rounded females. But as wife for a strong-willed man like her client? No way! He'd eat her for breakfast and forget her by lunchtime!

'Eye-catching, isn't she?' James continued. 'A beautiful eighteen-year-old virgin from an impeccable, wealthy family. What more could a man ask for?'

'He doesn't need the money!'

'Since when does needing it motivate millionaires? It's power they're after; linking one dynasty with another to make bigger and better conglomerates. And Lala's father heads one of the largest in the country.'

'So he's selling off one of his little assets?' Stephanie opined. 'Poor kid. She'd be better off with a man nearer her own age.'

'She'll be delighted to settle for Turkey's most eligible bachelor.'

'Being the richest doesn't make you the most eligible.'

Stephanie was being bitchy, but could not help it. There was something about Tariq that set her nerves on edge, like a knife scraping a plate. He only had to regard her with those piercing eyes of his, and she felt impaled by them; just had to come on site for her to gasp for air, as if he had created a vacuum around him.

His presence beside her was as unexpected as it was unwanted, and she jumped nervously, her bare arm brushing against his sleeve.

'If you can bear to tear yourself away from James,' he smiled down at her, 'my mother would like to meet you.'

It was impossible for Stephanie to refuse the command. Not that she had a chance to, for his hand was on the back of her chair, drawing it out. Was there no end to his presumption?

Except this wasn't a summons from the master, but a request from his mother. Nodding, she rose and accompanied him across the room to where sat the matriarch of the Hamid family.

Smiling faces turned to Stephanie as she and Tariq approached his table, the prettiest woman there being Lala, olive-skinned and sloe-eyed. She was truly a creature from the Arabian Nights, her only concession to modernity a halo of curls—almost a frizz—in place of the shining locks of a fairy-tale princess.

'So this is Miss Rodgers.' Mrs Hamid's voice was heavily accented, as she extended a hand. 'I am so pleased to meet you.'

Stephanie felt like a monkey on a stick, though unlike the monkey, she wasn't sure what she was expected to perform. There were smiles all round as she was introduced to everyone, then settled in a chair beside her hostess.

'My son's spoken a great deal about you,' Mrs Hamid said.

Stephanie threw him a swift glance, surprising a glint of amusement in his eyes.

'Only good things,' he assured her.

'Naturally,' his mother affirmed. 'The whole family is delighted with the Clinic. We found your design excellent.'

'It wasn't mine,' Stephanie corrected. 'Several of us worked on it, and Mr Lister had the final say.'

'But I understand you were responsible for the interior,' Mrs Hamid persisted. 'We were especially impressed at how cleverly you kept to the practical without sacrificing the traditional.'

'Stephanie thrives on challenge,' Tariq put in.

He had drawn up a chair next to her, sitting so close that had she moved her leg an inch it would have touched his. Again she felt the lack of air which his nearness always engendered, and drew a swift, silent breath. Not silent enough it seemed, for he noticed it.

'We mustn't embarrass Stephanie,' he went on. 'Compliments make the English uncomfortable.'

'Of course they don't.' Stephanie was not about to agree with him. 'But designing the Clinic was a team effort, as I said. One of us would put forward a suggestion, and after we'd batted it around a bit, the idea belonged to everyone.'

Mrs Hamid waved a bejewelled hand. 'No matter how it was achieved, the three designs you gave us were excellent. It was difficult knowing which one to choose.'

'Nevertheless, I think you made the right decision, Mama,' Tariq stated, and though he must have noticed Stephanie's startled expression, he let it pass.

Not so his mother, who gave her a keen look.

'As this Clinic is a memorial to my husband and my father-in-law,' she explained, 'Tariq insisted I had the final choice.'

Stephanie's eyes went to his, and the side of his mouth curved in a half-smile.

'Contrary to what you may think,' he murmured, 'I do allow women an opinion!'

Deciding silence was her best answer, Stephanie shrugged. However, Mrs Erim—who appeared young enough to be Lala's sister rather than her mother—put in mischievously, 'I hope you haven't been making things uncomfortable for Miss Rodgers?'

'Perish the thought!' Tariq said.

'Not till I've checked with the architect herself!' Mrs Erim's brown eyes twinkled at Stephanie. 'You shouldn't take him seriously. He doesn't mean half the things he says to us.'

Stephanie was wondering who Mrs Erim meant by 'us', when Mr Erim proudly informed her that his wife was a career woman too, and owned Elegance, one of the city's finest boutiques.

'You'll find me there every day,' the woman declared. 'It's not simply a hobby to give me couturier clothes at wholesale prices!' She gave Stephanie's dress the once-over. 'I see you went to my rival—but I'll forgive you!'

All eyes riveted to Stephanie and, sensing her embarrassment, Mrs Hamid took over the conversation.

'The little prayer house your firm submitted was a

charming idea too, Miss Rodgers. We were most taken with it.'

Stephanie was so startled by this that she forgot diplomacy. 'Then why was it turned down?'

'We didn't have the land on which to build it. But last week Tariq managed to acquire an adjoining piece, so we can now go ahead.'

'That's wonderful! I'm so pleased.'

A sanctuary, where patients and visitors could go for emotional succour, was an idea Stephanie had dreamed up herself, and she had devoted most of her spare time to its design. It wasn't a mosque—she could hardly see a woman being allowed to have a hand in one!—yet she had managed to give it the same feeling, and had been extremely disappointed when it had elicited no comment from the Hamid family. Now it appeared that lack of land rather than interest had been the reason.

'Was the prayer house also a team effort?' Mrs Hamid asked.

Stephanie nodded, though the swift colour that rushed into her cheeks was seen by Tariq's gimlet eye.

'So it was *your* idea,' he said into her ear. 'I should have guessed.'

'How?'

'Because of the use of colour. You chose your favourite ones—as in your dress.'

'You're very perceptive.'

'I'm glad you've noticed.'

'I always have.'

'Have you?' His eyes bored into hers. 'I think not.'

Even had they been alone, Stephanie wouldn't have challenged his comment, for there was an intimacy in it she was reluctant to explore. Reluctant? Who was she kidding? Downright afraid, if truth be told!

'Would it be difficult to make the prayer house slightly larger?' Mrs Hamid ventured.

'Not at all. It's simply a matter of drawing up new specifications and——'

'We've talked enough about work for one evening, Mama,' Tariq intervened impatiently. 'You'll have plenty of time to go over things with Stephanie. She'll be here several more months.'

'Only about two,' Stephanie said. 'After that, Mustafa will be supervising the day-to-day work and I'll fly back for a fortnightly inspection.'

'I'm not sure I'll agree to that,' came the autocratic response. 'If I consider your presence necessary, you will stay.'

This was neither the time nor place to argue, and Stephanie quickly turned away, disturbed to catch his mother eyeing her almost malevolently. If looks could kill, they'd be carrying me out feet first! she thought. Yet it can't be anything I've said . . . All at once she knew it had to do with Tariq.

Holy Moses! The woman imagined her high and mighty son was angling for an affair! Unexpectedly she saw the humour of it. It would serve him right if he fell for a foreigner—and a career woman to boot! A strong-minded, liberated lady could teach him a lesson or two! But not me, Stephanie decided grimly. The less I have to do with him the better. He might be great in bed—remembering his lovemaking the night they had returned from the Islands, she was pretty sure he was—but out of it he was a pain in the neck!

'I must be getting back to my table,' she murmured with a smile, and before Tariq could accompany her, hurriedly returned to James.

'Quite a lengthy royal audience.' He quirked an eyebrow at her. 'Is the flush on your cheeks triumph or anger?'

'Anger?'

'With our inestimable host.'

'Why should I be angry with him?'

'Because I get the impression he enjoys rubbing you up the wrong way.'

'Not this time,' she lied, feigning a smile as she saw Tariq watching her across the room. 'He was charm itself. Now, how about offering me a drink?'

'With champagne flowing like water, why not?'

'On second thoughts, let's take a turn in the garden. It's awfully hot in here.'

As she jumped to her feet, she heard the soft sound of tearing fabric. Dismayed, she saw she had caught the hem of her dress with her heel.

'Damn!' she muttered. 'I'd better stitch it before it goes further.'

Excusing herself, she went in search of needle and thread, which she found in a well appointed powder-room off the main hall.

She was busy fixing her hem when the door swung open and Lala drifted in on a cloud of pink organza.

'Oh dear!' she exclaimed prettily, hurrying forward. 'You haven't done anything disastrous to that gorgeous dress, have you?'

'Thankfully, no.' Stephanie bit off the end of her thread and smiled at her. 'I love *yours*. Is it from your mother's boutique?'

'No. Mama and I bought it in Paris. I adore shopping there, don't you?'

'Knightsbridge is more my scene,' Stephanie confessed. 'With a good dollop of Marks and Spencer!'

'I only know Harrods,' Lala giggled, seating herself at a mirror and dabbing powder on her nose. 'And Fortnum's, of course. I'm crazy about their chocolate mints! But I daren't eat too many or Mama gets cross.'

Stephanie rose and smoothed her skirt. What a lot of empty-headed chatter! Tariq deserved her! Or maybe she would suit him: a beautiful dummy he could treat like a doll!

'You have the most fantastic colour hair,' Lala went on, admiring it through the mirror. 'Is it natural?'

'To the roots and beyond!' Stephanie was more amused than irritated. 'Don't tell me you fancy changing yours?'

'Madly. But Mama would be livid if I did. The minute I marry, though, I'll dye it.'

'What if your husband prefers you as a brunette?'

'That's a tricky question! But I'm sure I'll find an answer.'

Forcing a smile, Stephanie went out, leaving Lala spraying scent behind her ears.

She was crossing the marble-floored hall when Tariq loomed from behind a pillar and barred her way.

In the bright light of the overhead chandelier, the pupils of his eyes were pinpoints of jet, the irises a warm chestnut-brown. Stephanie felt as if she were drowning in them—and resisting his sensual magnetism was like swimming in a sea of honey. But resist it she must if she valued her peace of mind. If only she were miles away from him—no, that he was holding her close, kissing her, touching her . . . God! she was going nuts!

'I thought you'd left,' he said, coming closer.

His nearness made her conscious of her body—her breasts tingling as she remembered his hands on them, her lips parting as if still savouring the taste of his mouth.

'I'd hardly go without James,' she managed to say.

'You are lovers?'

The blatancy of the question took her aback, and she stiffened angrily.

'Forgive me,' he apologised. 'I had no right to ask.'

'Damn right you didn't!'

Before he could answer, a portly man with a large cigar

puffed down on them, giving Stephanie the opportunity of escaping.

How dared Tariq ask such an intimate question! Did he think himself her keeper? That because she worked for him he could monitor her morals the way he did his sisters'?

Still fuming, she rejoined James, and sight of his smiling, uncomplicated presence decided her to say nothing about her encounter with Tariq.

'Sorry to be so long,' she apologised.

'No sweat. I got your drink.'

She saw the bottle of champagne in front of her. 'Just the thing to quench my thirst!'

Nursing their drinks, they watched the dancers. Almost as if magnetised, her eyes became riveted to Tariq, Lala in his arms. The girl seemed even tinier when held against him and, irritated by the sight of them, though she had no rational reason, Stephanie set down her glass and jumped up.

'Come on, James, let's dance. What are we waiting for?'

What indeed? she asked herself as he led her on to the floor. So she could watch Tariq more closely? Hear the sweet nothings he was probably whispering into the shell-like ear provocatively close to his lips?

With an effort she concentrated on James. With his calm manner and warm heart he would make a wonderful husband. But not for her. She needed someone stronger. Not that he was a weakling, but his amiable nature would allow her to walk all over him. Tariq, on the other hand, however much he loved a woman, would never let himself be ordered around.

Hell, why think of the Turk when James was so much nicer? But so much less exciting! Yet did she want excitement? As she resolutely turned from the answer,

James whirled her round and she found herself next to her host and Lala.

Pretending she hadn't seen him, she smiled at James as if he *were* her lover, and lifted her hand to trace the side of his cheek. He responded by holding her closer, which made her dislike herself thoroughly for leading him on, and she was glad when the music stopped and they could leave the floor.

If she didn't get out of here she'd scream! She glanced at her watch. It was only eleven, far too early to leave.

'How about that stroll you talked about?' James suggested.

Nodding, she went with him to the french windows. She would probably have to battle with an amorous advance, but that she could cope with. It was Tariq she didn't know how to handle!

'My dance, I think,' his softly accented voice said behind her.

Talk of the devil! Resolutely she refused to turn.

'I think not. I'm going out for some air.'

'It won't evaporate!'

He swung her round, and with a curt nod at James, led her back to the dance floor, encompassing her in a steely hold which left her breathless, literally and figuratively.

It might have been his heartbeat, his soft breath on her cheek, the special smell of him that was opiate to her senses, but Stephanie felt as if her bones were turning to jelly. She drew a deep, steadying breath, longing to escape and knowing that short of pummelling at him and making a spectacle of herself, she had no option but to stay. She was stuck with him and must pretend she was having a great time.

'Are you all right, Stephanie?'

He had to be joking! Quickly she assumed nonchalance. 'Why shouldn't I be?'

For an answer he tightened his hold and pressed her

against the hard length of his body. Oh God! She shut her eyes. Maybe if I meditate he'll disappear! Or how about some light conversation or telling him a joke? Joke with Tariq? That was a laugh in itself! I'm mad to let him, affect me like this. He's only dancing with me, for heaven's sake! It's just a mental aberration on my part that the scent of him, the texture of his skin on my cheek, is driving me crazy!

'Please take me back to James,' she whispered.

'You're still angry with me for asking if you were lovers?'

She ignored the question. 'I'm tired, Tariq. I've had a long day.'

'You're running away from me again.'

'Yes.'

'Why?'

'I can't relax with you,' she said directly.

'Am I so frightening, then?'

'Intimidating. We disagree on too many things and I don't like arguing with you.'

His laugh was abrupt. 'You could have fooled *me*.'

She said nothing, breathing a sigh of relief when he guided her back to her table.

'That was a short dance,' James smiled as Tariq walked away.

'Long enough for me.' She moistened her lips. 'I'm sorry to be a bore, but would you mind if we left?'

'Like that, eh?'

'Like what? Do stop reading things into nothing! I've a busy day behind me, and an even busier one ahead.'

'Right,' he said equably. 'Home it shall be.'

He jumped to his feet and, feeling piggish, but still determined to leave, Stephanie preceded him from the room.

CHAPTER FIVE

ON HER way to the Clinic next morning Stephanie stopped off at a florist to send a bowl of flowers and a thank-you note to Mrs Hamid. It irked her to say what a delightful evening she had had, but she could hardly admit that it had been a disturbing one!

Still, it had given her a glimpse of how the rich in Turkey lived—no different from the rich anywhere, it seemed—and how women in this pampered section of society were gradually merging into the twentieth century. Turkey, though predominantly Muslim, was not restrictively so—as in Iran and many Arab countries—and from what she had gleaned last night, women here held responsible posts in government, commerce, and the sciences. So much for Tariq's prejudice!

Of course there had been a backlash to this emancipation, with many of the young reverting to the old traditions while embracing a modern life-style. It was an uneasy mix of two opposing attitudes, and she did not see it happily co-existing for long. One or other would inevitably have to take precedence.

Yet Tariq still walked the middle path. Having adopted the tactics of the West to become a high-powered tycoon, he clung—where marriage and women were concerned—to the old ways. She wondered what family crises would have erupted had his sisters elected to follow a career, or his brothers not married the girls he had chosen for them.

And what about the lovely Lala, picked by his family to be his wife when he finally settled down? Would she have been *persona non grata* with him if, like her mother, she had chosen to run a shop?

Irritated to be thinking of him again—he seemed to stick in her mind like a burr—she was glad to reach her office and attend to the problems that had cropped up since yesterday.

By mid-afternoon her desk was clear and—miracle of miracles—she found herself at a loose end. She didn't fancy going home—it was too lovely a day—and she was too edgy to go sightseeing, so she plumped for the feminine thing and went window shopping! She might even take a peep at Mrs Erim's boutique.

Leafing through the directory for the address of Elegance, she found it was a few doors away from the shop where she had bought her dress for Tariq's party.

Some half-hour later she was strolling along Cumhuriyet Cadessi, gazing into windows of glittering jewellery and the latest in European clothes and accessories. The luxury of it all had her gasping, for the displays put even the most exclusive London boutiques in the shade.

Elegance was half-way down the street, and had an extremely modern front of steel and dark blue enamel. The starkly plain window displayed a single outfit only: a multi-coloured Missoni Suit. Two women were moving around inside the boutique, and as Stephanie went to walk on, one of them saw her and hurried to the door.

It was Mrs Erim, casually smart in a black silk shirt-waister with an abundance of gold chains and bracelets.

'Miss Rodgers! How nice to see you. Won't you come in for a coffee?'

Embarrassed, Stephanie shook her head. 'I was just passing.'

'Even so, can't you spare a few moments?' Mrs Erim was already drawing her inside to a chair, and taking the one opposite.

How like Lala she looked! She really could be taken for

her sister, Stephanie mused; more sophisticated though, with slightly heavier features and definitely more intelligence.

'Are you shopping or merely looking?' Mrs Erim asked easily, as a well groomed assistant served them coffee.

'Looking, I'm afraid. Though I must say the suit in your window's very tempting!'

'It is, isn't it! But I promise not to play—how do you call it?—devil's advocate.' Mrs Erim waved an arm, bracelets jangling. 'I'm so pleased I saw you through the window. I was going to get in touch with you, anyway. My husband and I are thinking of remodelling our apartment, and we wondered if you'd be interested in taking on such a small project?'

'The smallness of it wouldn't stop me,' Stephanie assured her. 'It depends how busy we are. I'll have to find out from Mr Lister.'

'I do hope you can do it. I've set my heart on having you.'

Had she indeed? Stephanie could not help being flattered. 'Even if I can't, I'll be happy to give you a few suggestions. Let's wait and see.'

Though disappointed at not having an instant 'yes', Mrs Erim was not one to give in.

'I've just had an idea,' she beamed. 'We're having a musical soirée Sunday evening, and if you're free to come—say at six o'clock—it would give you a chance to look around before the other guests arrive.'

Afraid Tariq would be there, Stephanie was about to say she had a date with James when she realised he might be going, too! Aware of the magpie-bright eyes scanning her face, and knowing she had hesitated too long for a refusal to sound anything but rude, she had no choice but to nod and accept the invitation.

For the rest of the week she debated whether to telephone Mrs Erim and plead a forgotten engagement.

But each time she picked up the telephone she chickened out. Anyway, why shouldn't she go and enjoy herself? She liked music, and a soirée sounded rather unusual. If Tariq was there and started riling her, she'd simply turn her back on him.

Promptly at six on Sunday, she entered the white and gold living-room of the Erims' triple-storeyed apartment. Wide glass doors opened out on to a magnificent terrace where small tables were set for the buffet supper that was to precede the recital, while in the room itself, sofas and armchairs had been pushed against the walls to allow dozens of gilt chairs to be placed in front of a small, raised dais.

'So pleased you managed to come early.' Mrs Erim proffered a silver salver of canapés, while her husband pressed a Buck's Fizz into Stephanie's hand.

'Just a drink, thanks,' she demurred, glad to find she felt at ease.

Maybe it was because she knew she looked particularly good in a black silk trouser-suit which made her appear taller than her five foot eight. Her hair was equally tailored, the red-gold strands swept back into a roll to frame her face. It was almost Victorian in its severity, except for the soft wisps she had let stray upon the ivory column of her neck and flick over the curve of her ears. It made her cheekbones stand out and drew attention to the full curve of her mouth, a scarlet splash of colour in a coolly aloof face.

'If you don't mind me taking my drink with me,' she said, 'I'd like to look around.'

She found each room lovelier than the next, and could not fathom why the Erims wanted to do any alterations. But clearly they were ripe for something new, though she still felt it was change for change's sake.

After a quick perusal, and a second, slower one, she began to have a better idea of what could be done, and suggested turning several small rooms into fewer larger ones, and building a glass-walled sitting-room on one of the upper terraces. But it was her idea of moving the staircase closer to the wall and turning the upstairs hall into a picture gallery that met with rapturous approval.

'I knew we were right to get expert advice!' Mrs Erim enthused. 'If you could go ahead and do the plans . . .'

'I'm afraid I can't take on the job,' Stephanie apologised. 'I spoke to Mr Lister on Friday and he wants me back in England as soon as I can leave the Clinic. If we agreed to do your apartment and it wasn't finished by then, it would mean my having to come back too often to supervise it.'

'Oh, dear! And I was so hoping . . .'

'I can still draw up my suggestions,' Stephanie volunteered. 'And I can highly recommend the contractors I'm using.'

'You're making me feel better already!'

The woman slipped an arm through Stephanie's, and returned with her to the main reception room as the first guests arrived.

Quickly the large room began to fill, though there was no sign of Lala—or Tariq, either. Maybe the Erims had only invited friends of their own age group? But as the thought crossed her mind, she glimpsed the girl, a vision in blue chiffon, with a *diamanté* belt clasping her tiny waist, and a matching one tied Indian fashion around her black curls.

The instant she saw Stephanie, she glided over to her. 'Mama said you'd be coming early and I meant to be ready. But it always takes me ages to dress!'

'A fault endemic in women,' Stephanie laughed.

'I don't understand that word, but I get the meaning!' Lala chattered on happily, though her eyes kept darting to the entrance hall until, in mid-sentence, she gave a *moue* of apology and rushed across the room.

No need to ask why. Sourly, Stephanie saw a wide-shouldered figure come into the room. Her heart did a wild tattoo and she reached for another Buck's Fizz from a passing waiter. Nothing like a bit of Dutch courage, she decided, gulping it down. Though why she should be afraid of Tariq, lord alone knew!

Mesmerised, she watched Lala catch his hand and gaze into his face like an adoring puppy. It was impossible to see his reaction for she only had a glimpse of his profile, though she noticed he didn't withdraw his hand from the small, clinging one.

Anxiously hoping to avoid him, Stephanie took the nearest chair and tried to merge into her surroundings. She was congratulating herself she had succeeded when a familiar tangy scent wafted towards her, and a dark voice spoke her name.

'Stephanie! What an unexpected pleasure.'

Calmly she tilted her head to meet Tariq's eyes, and from the corner of hers saw Lala waylaid at the far end of the room.

'Mr and Mr Erim wanted some professional advice, and as I also like music . . .'

'Then you're in for a wonderful evening. Yavez Kaya is a brilliant violinist.' He glanced around him. 'James with you?'

'No. I may be meeting him later.'

'I see.'

Stephanie was glad he didn't, and wished he would go away.

'May I help you to some food?' he asked.

He had said exactly the same at James's brunch party, and remembering how *that* day had ended, her cheeks became stained with flags of red.

'Please don't bother, thanks. I don't in the least mind being on my own.'

'I'm glad to hear it. But I was merely hoping you'd take pity on *me*.'

Knowing he was laughing at her, she followed him to the terrace and a table groaning with delicacies. All too aware of his trousered leg brushing her skirt as he reached for a plate and handed it to her, and of his fine-boned hand deftly pronging the food, she doubted whether she could eat anything, and helped herself to the smallest possible portions.

'Don't tell me you're dieting!' he exclaimed. 'Your figure's perfect as it is.'

'Which is why!'

'A kilo or two would improve it.'

'How can one improve perfection?' she mocked, and had the pleasure of seeing him grin.

'You've an answer for everything, haven't you?' He took her plate and piled it high.

'I'll never manage all that!'

Ignoring her protest, he took her elbow and guided her to a table in the corner. Predictably, Stephanie picked at her food, irritated that Tariq was eating with gusto. Still, why shouldn't he? As far as he was concerned he was only being polite to a professional acquaintance. So why couldn't she regard him in the same vein?

Because he's too sexually exciting, she admitted, and he's making me feel like a frustrated spinster! She was mulling over this none-too-pleasant thought, when Lala suddenly appeared.

'I've been looking all over for you, Tariq,' she announced breathlessly.

'I wasn't planning on running away,' he said indulgently as he drew up a chair and settled her in it. 'Catch your breath while I fetch you something to eat.'

There was much to be said for old-fashioned gallantry, Stephanie acknowledged, and remembered telling Tariq the danger of throwing out the baby with the bath water.

There was no denying the feminists had done exactly that, and were the poorer for it. Yet how difficult it was to know where to draw the line.

As Tariq moved off, Lala's liquid eyes homed in on Stephanie. 'Isn't he the darlingest man you've ever met?'

'Er—yes.'

'And so gorgeous-looking. I keep telling him he should be a film star.'

With an effort Stephanie kept a straight face. 'I bet he appreciated that.'

'He said it would bore him to death!' Lala giggled. 'He's terribly clever, you know. I often get nervous talking to him, but he says he enjoys being with me. I suppose it's because I know nothing about his work, and he finds me relaxing.'

Stephanie wasn't sure if the girl was being artless or warning her off. Except her eyes held no malice, their glow of pleasure innocent. Yet everything Lala said reaffirmed Stephanie's opinion that Tariq would eventually marry this pretty little creature who would place no demands on him mentally, and give him the adoration he considered his due.

Confirmation came later that evening while Yavez Kaya was playing a selection of Bach sonatas and partitas.

Immediately supper was over she had excused herself on the pretext of having to make an urgent phone call, and gone straight to the powder-room, where she had stayed until scraping chairs told her the concert was due to begin. Only then had she slipped back into the room and taken a seat near the door.

She was congratulating herself for having managed to stay as far from Tariq as possible, when the woman in front of her edged slightly to the left, putting him directly in her line of vision! Once again her heart lurched as she found herself staring at his profile: the springing jet hair, the dominant nose and chin. Lala was beside him—naturally—her curly black head barely reaching to his shoulder.

As the sound of Bach's Sonata No 3 filled the room, Stephanie willed herself to concentrate on the music. Soon she was lost in the creation of a genius, rendered by a genius. Here was none of the romanticism of Mozart, the torment of Beethoven, the vivacity of Vivaldi: simply the outpouring of a precise, logical mind touched by magic.

After the sonata came a partita, and Stephanie found her eyes straying back to the dark figure she had vowed to ignore. An arm rested across the back of Lala's chair, the hand partially hidden by a chiffon flounce. But it was the other hand that riveted her attention: lying idly on his lap, it lightly clasped a red-tipped one.

Blinding, burning jealousy swamped her and she hated herself for it. I'm out of my mind, she told herself desperately. She wasn't Tariq's keeper any more than he was hers, so what did it matter whose hand he held? Except it did! Not because she wanted him herself—therein lay disaster—but because it infuriated her that a man of his mental stature should consider tying himself to a girl with one tenth of his intelligence!

As the violinist took his final bow and the applause subsided, people broke into small groups. Hurriedly rising, Stephanie went over to the Erims and bade them goodnight, intent on escaping before Tariq saw her again.

Congratulating herself on having managed it, she fetched her wrap from the cloakroom and walked smack into him!

'We should really stop meeting like this!' she joked lightly, recollecting he had waylaid her in the same way at his party.

He ignored her attempt at humour. 'You were running

off without saying goodnight to me?'

'You were talking and I didn't like to interrupt you.'

'You could have waited till I stopped.'

'Was it so important we said goodnight to each other?'

His mouth thinned with anger. 'What is it with you, Stephanie? I thought we were friends.'

'We are. But only professionally.'

'What does *that* mean?'

'Once my work's finished here, we're unlikely to meet again.'

'You think so?' His eyes flashed dark fire. 'In the short time I've known you, you've consistently tried to speak for me. If ever I lose my voice, I'll know where to come! But, intelligent though you are, you are not infallible. And where I'm concerned you're invariably a hundred per cent wrong!'

'I'm sorry,' she said stiffly, moving to the elevator.

'So you should be! You go out of your way to rile me.'

'On the contrary. I go out my way to avoid you!'

'That riles me even more!'

Reluctantly she smiled. 'It seems whatever I do is wrong.'

'That's my tune, I think. You're a difficult woman to understand.'

'Don't try.'

'Perhaps it's because you don't understand yourself,' he went on softly. 'Maybe you're scared to.'

'Nonsense. I know myself very well.'

'Then why do you reject my friendship; why do you insist it's only professional?'

'Because it's safer that way.' Her answer came out before she could stop herself, and she saw his sardonic expression.

'So you're a woman who likes to play safe, eh?' His smile was wolfish. 'You disappoint me. I thought you had courage.'

'Don't you think it courageous of me to stand up to the great Tariq Hamid?'

'Foolhardy—as you will learn.'

'Are you threatening me?'

'You are your own greatest threat, Stephanie. Don't you know that running from something you fear only increases the fear? Stand up and face it. Sooner or later you'll have to.'

Sooner—rather than later—she would be in England, Stephanie reminded herself, giving him back stare for stare, determined not to let him see how unnerving she found him.

'When I spoke about safety just now,' she said, 'I was thinking of my job.'

'Your job?' He frowned. 'What does that have to do with our friendship?'

Hiding her elation at finding such a marvellous get-out, she presented it to him.

'Friendship can turn sour when two people hold opposing views on important issues, and I don't fancy running the risk of quarrelling with you and having you replace me here—as you once threatened to do. That's why I'd rather keep our relationship on a business footing.'

In the ensuing silence a shutter seemed to come down over the bronzed face. Had she been too blunt? But it had either been that or . . . She shied away from the alternative, reluctant to explore it.

'That's the second time you've made such accusation,' Tariq said slowly. 'I hoped I had reassured you, but it seems you can't accept my word . . .'

Haughtily he side-stepped her and pressed the elevator button.

For the few seconds it took to glide up to them, they stood together without speaking, though she was intensely conscious of his tightly reined anger.

The elevator door slid open and she stepped inside, hoping he wouldn't come down with her, and irrationally annoyed when he didn't.

'The porter will get you a taxi, Stephanie. A liberated woman like yourself would feel uncomfortable being escorted down!'

Face flaming, she was glad when the door closed, and she leaned shakily against the wall.

From now on she would monitor her invitations before accepting them, and if there was the slightest possibility of Tariq being present, she would stay home and knit!

CHAPTER SIX

DESPITE her resolve not to contact Tariq, Stephanie needed his approval for the colour schemes she and the interior decorator had devised for the patients' rooms.

A call to his secretary informed her he was busy with overseas visitors, and she had to wait two days until an appointment was arranged.

Remembering how acrimoniously they had parted, she was apprehensive at meeting him on his own. Had he been British or American—a culture she could understand—she would have let things take their natural course. But he was Turkish and incomprehensible to her, and she foresaw a host of pitfalls if she did not watch her step—which definitely had to be on the straight and narrow!

The instant she walked into his office and he rose from behind his desk to greet her, his face a composed mask, she knew she had worried needlessly. His eyes were like a stranger's, his manner punctilious.

So be it! If that was how he wanted it, she'd play him at his own game!

With an outward composure which in no way reflected her inner turmoil, she took a sheaf of coloured drawings from her briefcase and put them in front of him, explaining in a precise, colourless voice their various advantages and disadvantages.

'Blues and greens are cool colours and many people regard them as healing ones. But if you prefer warmer shades——'

'It's of no importance to me.' His tone signified she was wasting his time. 'You know your job, and I'm happy to leave this kind of decision to you.'

Feeling like a schoolgirl reprimanded by her teacher, Stephanie stuffed the drawings back into her briefcase.

'I'm sorry I bothered you. I was under the impression you wanted to approve everything.'

'In the beginning, yes. But not since I've had the opportunity of watching you work.'

From anyone else this would have been a compliment, but Tariq said it so casually she felt he was merely paying lip service to politeness, a feeling which intensified as, without waiting for her response, he turned away and picked up the telephone.

For an instant she remained where she was, thinking he had more to say, but as he started speaking Turkish she realised that their meeting was at an end, and quietly walked out.

She was aflame with temper. If he had wanted to show her where she stood with him, couldn't he have done it with a bit more subtlety? Pity she hadn't told him so! Except that if she had, he would have known his attitude had hurt her, and she would swallow her tongue before giving him that satisfaction!

There was only one thing to do: admit he was not only an impossible man to avoid, but an impossible man to know!

It was stupid to have thought anything else. Their first meeting should have warned her they had nothing in common other than sexual attraction. That was something she couldn't refute. Nor could he, if he were honest. His coldness to her today proved it. It was almost as if he had elected to play a role and had no intention of deviating from it.

Which suited her fine!

A few days later she stepped out of her office and saw him striding towards her accompanied by a grey-haired man in his forties.

'Ah, Stephanie. I'd like you to meet Dr Orgun. He's going to be our medical director.' Tariq's square-jawed face was expressionless, his punctilious manner relegating their relationship to the professional. 'I'm showing him around.'

She nodded. 'I'll be in the office if you want me.'

'We want you now. I'm sure Dr Orgun has many questions, and you can answer them far better than I can.'

'Not too many,' the doctor smiled, his English as excellent as Tariq's, though more accented. 'Don't forget, I've studied the plans.'

Tariq moved to the stairs, signalling her to join them. Whether intentionally or not, he remained on the other side of the doctor, chatting to the man as though totally unconcerned by her presence.

So what else was new? she thought ruefully. *She* might have spent all week stewing over his curtness to her, but quite clearly he hadn't given *her* a thought since she had left his office.

For the next hour the three of them went on a detailed tour of the building, and though Tariq frequently brought her into the conversation, he looked through her rather than at her.

But she still gave an Oscar-winning performance of not giving a damn as she walked with the two men along the concrete corridors—soon to be covered with acoustic tiles—to the topmost floor where the radiology and physiotherapy departments were to be situated.

Here Dr Orgun spent the most time, pacing out the rooms and making notes as to where he wished the electrical equipment placed.

'Although I'm a general physician,' he explained to Stephanie, 'I'm particularly interested in osteopathy and massage—a result of playing rugger in England!'

'A healthy body leads to a healthy mind,' Tariq grinned at him.

'Not always, my friend. Nor is the corollary true. If we——' A high-pitched bleep from his pocket cut him short. 'How time flies! I'm afraid I must go—I've a patient waiting. Don't bother seeing me off if you've other things to discuss.'

He went down the stairs at a run, leaving Stephanie feeling as if marooned on a desert island with an enemy.

'I don't think we have anything further to discuss,' Tariq stated, and, not giving her a chance to reply, strode after the doctor.

Blind with anger, she hurried to get ahead of him. For two pins she would call John and insist he replace her!

He almost had to, for next moment she found herself teetering on the edge of an empty lift shaft—the ground six giddying floors below!

'*Allah!*'

Arms lunged out as she swayed sickeningly, gripping her like steel bars and pulling her back so roughly her shoulder scraped hard against a concrete pillar.

'What the *hell* do you think you're doing?' Tariq rasped. 'You could have been killed!'

Dumb with fright, Stephanie stared at him. Then she began shaking, but not so much that she couldn't tell he was shaking too, shuddering as though with fever and breathing hard, his face ashen as a corpse!

'Of all the damn fool things to do!' he raged on. 'Haven't you the sense to watch where you're going on a building site? You, of all people!'

His fury engulfed her, and the full horror of what could have happened sank in. Her legs buckled beneath her, and he dragged her up and held her tightly. She sagged against him like a rag doll, totally incapable of moving. Nausea filled her, and she swallowed hard and took several gulps of air.

'We'd better get you down,' he said thickly. 'Can you walk or shall I carry you?'

'No—I mean, yes—I can walk!'

With an effort she straightened away from him and moved to the stairs. But she was still trembling, and seeing it, he placed a hand beneath her elbow and a firm arm around her waist.

Slowly they went down the stairs, neither of them speaking. As they reached the ground floor and she turned towards her office, he pulled her back.

'No more work for you today, Stephanie. I'm taking you home.'

The softness of his tone, unlike his earlier harsh one, brought tears of weakness to her eyes, showing her she was still in a state of shock. Hurriedly she blinked them away in case he noticed.

'Cry if you want to.'

Dammit, he had noticed! 'N-no, I'm f-fine.'

A crisp white handkerchief was thrust into her hand. 'Dr Orgun would say tears are a release of tension, and I'd agree with him.'

Even so she refused to give way to them, mutely following him to his car and leaning back against the soft leather seat as he drove the short distance to May's house.

'A hot bath and straight to bed,' he ordered, pulling into the kerb. 'Ask May to give you some coffee. The sweeter the better.'

'She isn't here,' Stephanie heard herself say as from a distance. 'She's in the States on a book tour . . . for a month.'

Before he could help her out of the car, she slipped from the passenger seat, but hardly had her feet touched the ground when he was beside her.

'Sure you can manage on your own?'

'Perfectly.' She mounted the steps and unlocked the

front door. 'It was kind of you to bring me back.'

'It was the least I could do.'

His hooded eyes were intent on her, and his mouth moved as if he were about to speak. Then thinking better of it, he gave a slight inclination of his head and returned to his car.

A hot bath and two cups of strong coffee later—sweet as Tariq had ordered—Stephanie felt back in the land of the living. The events of the past hour were taking on the shape of a half-remembered nightmare, something she could think about yet distance herself from, as if it had happened to someone else.

All she could recollect with any degree of clarity was Tariq's fury, though she was still unable to fathom why he had been so angry. He had acted as if she had wanted to fall down the lift shaft! Had he been worried by the publicity her death would have caused? She could almost see the screaming headlines: 'Young British Architect Dives to Death in Front of Turkish Tycoon . . . was he client or rejected lover?'!

She half smiled. No wonder he had been livid!

She chuckled, a startling sound in the silent room. How peaceful it was here, and how lucky she was to be living in this lovely old house. Yet how ungrateful she had been when Tariq had found it for her!

Curling up on the settee, the folds of her peach housecoat around her, her mind began to drift. England and home . . . Turkey . . . an alien country that was beginning to exert a strange pull on her.

The soft burr of the telephone stopped her mental wanderings. Let it ring. She was in no mood for small talk, and definitely not business talk with London! Whoever it was would have to call back tomorrow.

The ringing stopped and she sighed with relief. In a little while she would rustle up the energy to make herself another drink and go to bed. She had bought some

English paperbacks and there was a Forsythe she fancied reading.

The phone rang again and she glared at it, willing it to stop. But it went on relentlessly, and with a sigh she leaned across the back of the settee and lifted the receiver.

'How are you?'

The deep, rich voice nearly made her drop it.

'F-fine. Good as new, actually. There's no need to be concerned.'

'Naturally. My architect nearly falls six floors to her death before my eyes, and I'm expected to shrug it off!'

'*I* have.'

'You're cool, calm and British. *I'm* an emotional Turk!'

'Then as a cool, calm Briton I should have remembered lift shafts are a hazard. They make the best disaster movies!'

'When the movie's nearly a reality,' he bit out, then muttered something in Turkish. 'I don't suppose you did as I told you?' he resumed, his tone softer.

'You suppose wrong. I obeyed your commands implicitly.'

'Will it always take a near brush with death for you to do as I ask?'

'I do what I consider right,' she countered.

There was a pause before he spoke. 'What's your programme now?'

'Another hot drink, then bed.'

'You should eat something.'

'Yes, sir. I'll have breakfast tomorrow!'

'Have a good night, then.'

The line went dead, and she slowly replaced the receiver and leaned back against the settee. Silence settled around her once more, and again she was conscious of being alone in this large, empty house. Not afraid, though. The doors and windows were stout and well secured, and her bedroom had a double lock. She wasn't really worried. Just very much alone and slightly sorry for herself. Not that there was any necessity for it: a quick call to James and he'd come running.

Trouble was she didn't fancy seeing him, for it would mean recounting her horrific experience—which she'd rather forget.

Gradually the sky darkened, the pink and orange streaks turning to rose and violet, then purple and midnight-blue. Idly she switched on a lamp, reluctant to go foraging for food or put on the kettle for the drink she had promised herself.

It had been thoughtful of Tariq to check and see how she was. She had not expected him to, and was pleased he had. She closed her eyes, drifting into the borderland between waking and sleeping, unaware of the passing of time, of the warm air growing cooler, the lights on the Bosporus glowing brighter as the night deepened and the stars came out.

The peal of the front doorbell brought her to her feet, heart thumping. It was unlikely to be anyone for May—her friends knew she was in the States—nor could it be James, for he never arrived without warning. Frowning, she went to the entryphone outside her door.

'Who is it?' She kept her tone deliberately firm.

'Tariq.'

Relief flooded her, and her hand shook as she pressed the entry button and moved to the top of the stairs. She turned on the downstairs light, giving her a clear view of him as he came in, almost as if he were on a stage.

She had never thought he would visit her, and pleasure filled her as he smiled up at her and mounted the stairs. How handsome he was! How devastatingly physical! Surreptitiously she clutched at the banister. She should never have let him in. There were any number of excuses she could have made: that she was too tired . . . that she was in bed and he had woken her . . .

Yes, that was exactly what he had done! Woken her to the reality of her emotions: forced her to acknowledge the truth of her feelings.

At last she understood why his presence always agitated her, why his coldness infuriated her, his rare compliments delighted her. It was more than the response of a young woman to a powerful, attractive man: more than a primeval sexual urge that cried out to be appeased by him. It was love! That often illogical, irrational emotion that hit you like a thunderbolt—as it had hit her!

She was in love with Tariq Hamid.

For weeks she had refused to admit it, but she could no longer do so, any more than she could stop breathing. She loved his fine mind—even if she didn't always go along with what he believed: his old-world courtesy, his dynamic energy and ability, his humour, his—oh! the list was endless and unimportant, anyway. Who knew why one loved!

He reached her side, and only then did she notice he was carrying a hamper.

'I've brought you a snack,' he announced, looming large on the narrow landing. 'Caviar, chicken, champagne, peaches.'

'Only a *snack*?' She laughed. 'How mean of you!'

She led the way into the sitting-room, and in the glow of the single standard lamp he studied her.

'You're looking better.'

'I feel it.'

She started switching on the other lamps, and he unpacked the hamper, setting out the food on a tray before uncorking the champagne and filling the crystal goblet he had brought with him. Silent as a panther he came over and placed it in her hand, then pushed her gently down on the sofa, rested the tray on her lap, and settled himself in an armchair opposite.

She lifted her fork, but was so conscious of him, her hand shook.

'Relax, Stephanie.' He reached out and steadied it with warm fingers. 'I'm here to feed you, not seduce you!'

'I never thought otherwise.'

'That's no compliment to either of us!'

'Oh?'

'Either you're too unattractive to warrant masculine attention, or I'm not sufficiently masculine to be aware of you!'

'I didn't mean that, and you know it.' She tried to sound unconcerned, and marvelled she could manage it. 'I was merely letting you know I—I feel safe with you.'

'Not *too* safe,' he said suavely.

'I hope you don't mean that, Tariq. I'd hate having to defend my honour by hitting you with a chicken leg!'

His chuckle reverberated through the room. 'You're back on form, I see. I shall have to watch out for myself.'

So shall I, Stephanie thought despairingly, for now that the scales of delusion had fallen from her eyes, she saw exactly what he meant to her and where she had been heading these past frustrating weeks.

CHAPTER SEVEN

CURLED up on the sofa a little later, replete with food and sipping a second glass of champagne, Stephanie assessed the man opposite her as if seeing him for the first time.

And she was. Here was a Tariq she barely knew, a Tariq who was making her laugh and forget herself with him. She almost stretched herself like a cat, she felt so relaxed.

'What made you take up architecture?' he asked unexpectedly.

It was a question she had not thought he would ask, for until now he had shown little interest in her motivations.

'I like building things. I began with coloured blocks, went on to my brother's Lego, and here I am—designing clinics and hospitals!'

'And you're happy doing it?'

'I'd be happier designing houses and dealing with people rather than committees.'

'Committees *are* people!'

'Don't you believe it! Once people are on a committee they become pompous, priggish and pretentious. Of course, I'm generalising,' she added hastily.

'Don't bother being diplomatic,' Tariq said amusedly. 'I'm not one for committees either.'

'That doesn't surprise me. You're a committee unto yourself!'

He laughed outright. 'And I never answer myself back either, no matter how priggish, pompous and pretentious I am! But let's get back to you. When you say you'd prefer designing houses, I have the impression you don't mean millionaires' mansions!'

'You can say that again. The opposite in fact—sheltered housing.'

'What's that?'

'Homes for the elderly. Houses and apartments with wardens *in situ* to take care of them.'

'Ah, sheltered housing.' He appeared to mull over this. 'You won't find such words in *our* dictionary.'

'They're bold and clear in ours.'

He pulled a face. 'Another of your Western innovations? Segregating the old and having them cared for by strangers so they don't become a burden on their families? In my country, such a thing is unheard of. If parents can't cope on their own, their children take them in.'

'That's not an ideal solution, either,' Stephanie defended. 'Parents shouldn't be expected to be unpaid housekeepers and baby-sitters, which often happens when they live with their children.'

'Then their children need re-educating! Parents enjoy being used—as long as it's not abused! Put them into sheltered homes, and you segregate them into a world of the old.'

'Sheltered houses aren't prisons! Quite the opposite. They enable old people to retain their independence and not feel beholden to their families.'

'You've made out a good case, Stephanie, but I prefer *our* way.'

'You always do!' Afraid she had been too sharp, and not wishing to ruffle the tranquil atmosphere between them, she said quickly, 'I suppose it's basically a difference of culture.'

'Exactly. But three-quarters of the world think as we do! It's the northern races who are hard-hearted!'

'That's unfair,' Stephanie protested. 'It also has a lot to

do with the size of the family. It's easier when there are several children to share the caring. But where you have a one-child family, or at best two, the responsibility usually devolves on the daughter, if there is one.'

'I'll grant you that,' Tariq conceded. 'Though what you're actually doing is making out a good case for large families!'

She laughed, and his echoing smile revealed white teeth gleaming against a golden-brown skin.

'I see you don't intend arguing with me tonight, Stephanie, even though I know you consider me inflexible.'

'Steadfast,' she corrected demurely.

He laughed outright. 'Steadfast in my refusal to discard the tried and trusted old ways for the new?'

'Such as arranged marriages,' she said daringly.

'Why not? Their rate of failure is no higher—in fact less so—than your so-called Western "love match".'

Stephanie hesitated, longing to pose the question uppermost in her mind. Heck! Why not? She had nothing to lose.

'Would you have allowed your parents to choose *your* wife for you?'

'My father died when I was a child,' came the smooth reply.

'That's no answer! What about your grandfather? I understand *he* was head of the family.'

'Clearly I didn't always listen to him! Hence my still being single at thirty-four.'

'What about you and Lala?' The words slipped out, and seeing his expression freeze, she wanted to kick herself. 'I'm sorry, that was unpardonably personal. It's simply that I—I assumed there was an understanding between you.'

'A "hope" rather than an understanding,' came the flat

response. 'And not of my doing, I assure you. It was dreamed up by my mother and Lala's grandmother when Lala was a child.'

His answer said nothing—or everything, leaving open a question she desperately wanted answered. Did he or didn't he intend marrying the nubile Turkish girl?

'Not that I'll stay single much longer,' he added. 'Within a year I'll have to settle down. It's expected of me.'

'Do you always do what's expected? Don't you ever get the urge to throw your cap over the windmill?'

'Gravity will always bring it down! Which is why I'm a conformist, accepting only the tried and tested—like marriage. It's the mainstay of our culture because it works better than anything else.'

'Especially arranged marriages!' Stephanie teased, and didn't like it when he nodded.

'Love can blind you to a person's faults,' he said, 'and you can all too easily convince yourself it's possible to change them, though logic proves you rarely can! When parents do the choosing, they have more realistic considerations in mind than—than——'

'Bedability?'

'I couldn't have put it better myself!'

Leaning back in his chair, he focused on a spot above her head, as he had done the first time they had met—funny she should remember it!

'I often think I'd like a wife who can share my thoughts as well as my bed,' he went on.

'Really?'

'Of course.' Quizzically he regarded her. 'Why should that astonish you?'

'Because I can't imagine you sharing your thoughts and feelings with anyone—especially a female!'

'Although a woman is different from me physically

and emotionally, it doesn't mean she's my inferior. I just believe she'd be happier if she acknowledged those differences.'

'And happier still if she stayed home and waited on her lord and master!'

'Why not? Unless she has a God-given talent that should be utilised.'

'I can't believe I'm hearing this!' Stephanie clapped her hands to her ears. 'You're trying to rile me. You can't be serious!'

'Only partly,' he confessed with a grin. 'You're so positive in your views, I enjoy baiting you. Mind, to be honest, I do admit times are changing and women with it.'

'They've already changed. It's the men who haven't!'

'Can you blame us? It's bad enough competing with our own sex, but to compete with women . . .!' He gave a mock groan. 'Heaven preserve us!'

'You're already preserved—in the eighteenth century!'

He flung back his head and laughed, his strong throat swelling with the sound. 'I hope you fall in love with such a man! It will serve you right.' He laughed again, then leaned forward and stared at her. 'What would you do if you did?'

What indeed? Thank heavens he didn't know that what he saw as a joke was already an actuality, and no joke to her. A disaster more likely. But since he had posed the question, she must answer it.

'I'd hope his love for me would allow him to compromise. That's usually the basis for a happy marriage, isn't it?'

'Would *you* be willing to compromise?'

Tariq's eyes were dark with intensity, or was it because they were shadowed by the eyebrows frowning above them? Stephanie wished she knew if he were teasing or serious. Regardless, she'd take his question at face value.

'I'd like to think both parties were prepared to compromise,' she said slowly. 'Though women, being more emotional—on which point I'm sure you'll agree!—generally do most of the compromising!'

'Not if the woman was you!'

'I'm not as obstinate as you think.'

'Indeed? When was the last time you gave in on anything important?'

'I haven't so far,' she confessed. 'I guess I've been lucky.'

'Lucky,' he echoed. 'Yes, you were extremely lucky today. When I saw you teetering on the edge of the shaft . . .' He closed his eyes at the memory, his hooded lids masking the expression in the warm brown irises.

'I'm not irreplaceable,' she said lightly.

'To me you are.'

His words fell into the silence like fireballs on hay. She tried to hold herself aloof from the emotions he was sparking inside her, but it would have been easier to control a leaf in a tornado!

Their eyes met, the glow in his making her remember they were alone in the house, only a few feet apart: that he had only to reach out to touch her . . .

Oh no, she prayed. Don't let him do it! I'll be lost for ever, if he does.

Miserably she asked herself why it had to be Tariq and not James, or any other of the attractive men she had met in the past few years. Was it because he represented a challenge—a fortress to be stormed? It might well be why he desired *her*! Her very stubbornness, her refusal to kowtow to him, could act on him as a sexual stimulus.

'No,' she said agitatedly, not realising she had spoken aloud till the sound trembled between them.

'Yes,' he countered heavily. 'I'm afraid the answer is

yes. I've done everything in my power to fight against it, but I can't any longer.'

He rose and paced the room. Gone was the quiet panther, in its place a raging one who resented being prisoner of his emotions.

'It's the last thing I wanted!' he exclaimed. 'No, I'm lying! When you came into my office that first morning and glared at me so defiantly, I had a hunch it might end like this.'

'It's ended by our becoming friends,' she said hurriedly, aware of the vortex beckoning her, and not daring to let herself be drawn into it.

'*Allahin belasi*—dammit!' he swore vehemently. 'I'm not talking of friendship, I'm talking of wanting you, hungering for you!'

Wanting, hungering, but no mention of loving! Did he regard her as a chattel for his taking? An idiot without a mind of her own, and he a marauding conqueror to drag her off to his lair? From the look on his face, he seemed to think she'd be delighted by the prospect!

Anger robbed her of speech. And a good thing too, for she might have said more than she should.

'I can see you don't regard what I said as a compliment,' he pronounced.

'Clever of you to guess.' She fought to control her temper. 'I'm not a sex object, Tariq, whatever you may think. I have feelings, opinions, and above all the right to say no! Can you understand that word coming from a woman, or do the ones in your circle always say yes?'

'Yes.'

'My God!'

'You asked, and I've answered you.' The sable eyes glittered. 'I'm neither lying nor boasting—merely being honest—which a woman of your honesty should appreciate!' He lifted a hand. 'No, let me finish. The women in my past are past. It's you I'm concerned with now.'

'My answer's still no!'

His mouth tightened. 'When I said I wanted you, Stephanie, I didn't mean it as an insult.'

'It's no compliment to be regarded as a sex object,' she repeated.

'Surely it pleases you to know I desire you: that your face is before me night and day, your voice in my ears when I listen to music, when the soft wind blows through the palms. I can't get you out of my thoughts, and I want to be your lover.'

Heck! No one could accuse him of beating around the bush. Stephanie's anger dissolved—what woman could have sustained it in the face of such a declaration? Indeed, any Englishman in the same situation would as easily give vent to such feelings as a bull a calf!

But it didn't mean she was ready to fling herself into his arms—though the tempation was great. With an effort she pushed it from her mind. Did she genuinely want more than he was offering? Considering how different their ideas were, wasn't an affair enough? And what a fantastic lover he'd be! Tender yet passionate, demanding yet giving, warming her with the heat of his desire. So why not take what he offered, even if it only meant a temporary heaven?

The answer to her question brought her down to earth fast. She wanted permanence.

What she felt for Tariq was no ephemeral desire that could be dissipated by a few weeks or months of lovemaking. The admission was frightening and dismaying, and she stared at his wide-shouldered figure, conscious of how overwhelming her feelings were for this intelligent, amusing, but oh, so impossible man!

'Is there any chance of your forgetting what I said?' Tariq asked unexpectedly, crossing the room to kneel beside her.

'Forgetting?'

'Yes. Think of it as the ravings of a lunatic, and let us begin again.'

She wasn't sure what he meant. 'Begin what?'

'Getting to know one another. Giving ourselves a chance of becoming friends, and seeing where it leads us.'

Into his damned bed was what he hoped, though he knew better than to say it again. How cunning he was!

'And after we're friends, Tariq, what then? The pounce?'

'Never. Whatever happens between us will be because we both want it.'

She closed her eyes, terribly afraid he'd see she wanted it this very minute! He leaned closer and she clenched her hands to stop them reaching out to caress the silkiness of his hair, to stop her resting her cheek upon his and breathing in the fragrance of his breath.

'Please let's be friends,' he reiterated, 'and see where it takes us.'

She almost laughed in his face. She had heard of two minds with but a single thought, but here were two minds with diametrically opposed ones! Sex in his, love and marriage in hers.

Carefully she pondered the situation. If she accepted his offer, would propinquity help his feelings to deepen? After all, if simply meeting him professionally had enabled her to penetrate his armour to the extent she had, how much further might she go when his defences were down? Hell! It was an opportunity worth taking.

'I shouldn't have rushed you,' he muttered. 'I can see you don't trust me. But I give you my word I'll never take advantage of you.'

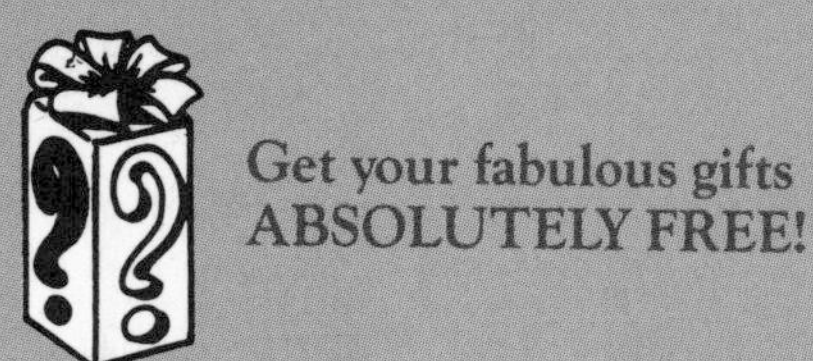

HARLEQUIN HOME READER SERVICE®

FREE OFFER CARD

4 FREE BOOKS

FREE DELIVERY

Place YES
sticker here

FREE FACT-FILLED NEWSLETTER

FREE SURPRISE

Please send me 4 Harlequin Presents® novels, free, along with my surprise gifts as explained on the opposite page.

108 CIH CANE

Name ______________________________
(PLEASE PRINT)

Address ______________________ Apt ________

City ______________________________

State ____________________ Zip ________

Offer limited to one per household and not valid for present subscribers.
Prices subject to change.

PRINTED IN U.S.A.

What about *her* taking advantage of him, she thought ruefully, when the mere touch of his fingers sent passion spiralling through her? And how reliable was *his* self-control, anyway? Remembering their return from the Islands, and how passionately he had kissed her, she nearly asked him!

'So?' he asked, his hand tilting her chin. 'As the auctioneers say, this is my third and final offer. Will you look on me as a friend and come out with me?'

Their eyes met, and an electric current sparked between them. She gasped, the sound muffled by the deep murmur in his throat as the tip of his finger traced a slow path down her cheek to the curve of her neck and the fragile hollow where a pulse beat erratically.

His eyes, dark with passion, roamed her face with a slow sensuality as erotic as a touch, and though she tried to look away, she was held in thrall by his magnetism, the powerful, primeval urge of a man for a woman. Involuntarily her eyes pleaded with him to forget promises and take her in his arms, kiss away her protests and love her with every breath in his body.

His response was instant, his need undeniable as, heart against heart, he drew her close and lowered her to the cushions. Fiercely his tongue parted her lips, probing and drinking the sweetness within, and letting her taste his own. Moaning, she clung to him, all logic gone as she held him tight and savoured the moment.

His thighs were sinewy and heavy upon hers, the swell of his arousal an urgent plea for satisfaction as he feverishly undid the buttons of her housecoat to fondle her breasts. They pulsed with desire, and his hands cupped their fullness as his lips traced a feverish path to her nipples, clasping them between teeth and tongue to lick and nip them into tingling points of longing.

Shakily she caressed his head, running her hands over

his hair and down the firm neck, aching for the fulfilment of total surrender, yet conceding how empty it would be without his love.

'No!' she cried, and agitatedly pushed him away.

For an instant he resisted, then he raised his body from hers and swung his legs to the ground.

'So much for my promise not to touch you!' he said flatly, raking back his hair and striding swiftly to the door. 'I'll go before you throw me out. I deserve no better.'

'Tariq, don't!'

If he left feeling guilty, their relationship would never develop. Besides, she was equally culpable, for the longing she had let him read in her eyes had acted on him like pollen to a bee.

'We both lost our heads,' she whispered, hurriedly sitting up and rebuttoning her housecoat. 'But I'm still prepared to—to go out with you.'

'You mean it?' He swung round on her, eyes alight.

'Yes.' She meant far more, but dared not say it: was almost afraid to think it. 'For the—for the rest of my stay here,' she went on unsteadily, 'I'll enjoy your friendship.'

'And I yours.'

Which makes both of us first-class liars! Stephanie thought, and wondered which one of them would prove the winner.

CHAPTER EIGHT

THOUGH she knew she was playing with fire, Stephanie did not regret her decision to go out with Tariq.

'I'm glad you haven't let my one mistake spoil things between us,' he had said, before leaving her apartment.

She had marvelled that he could kid himself they would remain friends and nothing more, but had not said so, remembering cause and effect, and dreading the effect on her if she scared him off by giving him an inkling of her hopes for their future.

Was she basing those hopes on reality or fantasy? In the long hours of the night, after he had left, she had mulled over their every meeting, trying to remember what he had said, how he had looked. The more she did, the more convinced she became that he loved her and was fighting marriage. That was why she was staking everything on her nearness being his undoing, and hoped he would have the courage to finally acknowledge that what he felt for her was more than a passing sexual fancy.

Or perhaps it wasn't a question of courage. Perhaps he genuinely did not realise how he felt about her. After all, for him to love someone like herself meant discarding many of his die-hard beliefs, and he could well be hoping that getting her into his bed would get her out of his system!

Not that he gave any indication of this in the ensuing weeks. In fact his behaviour was exemplary. Never did he put a foot wrong or a hand where it shouldn't be!

What was more, he was truly a marvellous friend and companion, and as a guide, incomparable. She had thought she knew Istanbul well, but through his eyes saw the city anew. Not surprisingly, for this was his home, and his pride in it boundless, his knowledge endless.

She had visited the Blue Mosque many times, enchanted by the stained glass windows and shining azure tiles. But with Tariq it became an entirely new experience for her, and, listening to him tell her its history—how vivid he made it compared with her guidebook!—she was able to envisage the millions who, over the aeons, had prayed here to their God.

The centuries-old covered bazaar she had pushed her way through endless times came alive as Tariq cleared a path for her along narrow lanes packed with buyers and vendors. With expert eye he pried out inexpensive treasures which Stephanie, in all her searches, had missed: minute sandalwood boxes inlaid with ivory; carved figures in wood; a coffee set encrusted with red and green stones too tiny to roughen the lips, yet glittering with life even in the dim light of the bazaar.

But the trinkets did not intrigue her so much as Tariq's wily buying of them. That he intended to haggle went without saying—not to have done would have lowered him in the merchant's estimation—but there was no curt offer from this well-bred Turk, nor a take-it-or-leave-it about-turn.

Open-mouthed she watched the two men dance a skilful minuet, a step by step lowering of the price: the merest flick of an eyebrow to show that if it weren't met, the dance was over. Gradually the price went down and down, until finally, with what she regarded almost as clairvoyance, both parties knew when rock bottom had been reached, and the bargain was struck.

Long ago, she had asked James what made Tariq tick, but nothing gave her a clearer indication than the three enchanted weeks of their friendship.

Intent on showing her that Istanbul was not representative of Turkey, he drove her into the vast open spaces beyond it. Here was the Turkey of the history books: ageless, rooted in the soil, seemingly untouched by progress.

No split levels or skyscrapers here; only beehive mud huts, cave dwellings and wooden houses. Jean-clad girls belonged only on television: real women were shrouded bundles, eyes hidden behind the veil as they shopped for food among the colourful merchandise spilling on to dusty pavements.

Here and there the modern did intrude: the panniers of a donkey stacked high with detergent powder, stalls where rolls of brightly coloured polyester lay side by side with black veils and voluminous cotton pantaloons, a one-pump garage whose owner arrived for work on a camel!

Beyond the villages lay a vista of barren countryside, where Tariq frequently paused to let a child shoo cattle off a dust-clouded road. On the grassy slopes shepherds kept their ancient vigil; below them farmers tilled with the plough, their women bent low over potato and onion patches, while their goats chomped the earth.

The change to vineyard and orchard was abrupt, and the eye feasted on mountain and stream, and lush valleys where the machine had edged itself behind the plough, and man-made fertiliser had taken the place of manure.

'Who'd want to live in a city when they can have all this?' Stephanie sighed blissfully one afternoon as she leaned an arm on the open window of the car.

'It's a harder life than it looks.'

'At least it's peaceful and non-competitive.'

'That appeals to you?'

She grinned. 'We all have our dreams!'

'I'm sure you'd have no trouble turning yours into reality.'

'Probably. Except it might end up more of a nightmare! You're right, Tariq. Living here looks idyllic, but on a permanent basis . . .'

'You change your mind fast,' he teased.

'I know. I suppose what it really amounts to is that I'd like the best of both worlds! A career as well as the opportunity of opting out when I wish.' She leaned forward to wave to a group of children at the roadside, leaving him to consider what she had said.

'Why haven't you married?' he asked her a few days later as they sat at a pavement café in Istanbul.

'I was too busy working.'

'You've been in love?' he probed, squinting at her in the sunlight.

'Oh, yes . . . with my dancing teacher when I was three!'

'And at twenty-three?'

She saw he was serious. 'With a fellow architect, actually.'

Deliberately she threw a pigeon some cake crumbs from her plate, knowing Tariq was waiting to hear more, and counting on the fact that he would hate it when he did! He might profess to be her friend, but she would bet a dime to a dollar that in a man of his type, jealousy lay close to the surface, waiting to rear its head.

'Tell me about him,' he said, leaning back in his chair. He was jacketless, his blue voile shirt showing the dark whorls of hair on his chest.

'It was such a long time ago,' she demurred. 'It's unimportant now.'

'Not to me. I want to know everything about you.'

She hid a smile. 'Well, as I said, he was an architect—we met at college—and we had all sorts of grandiose schemes to change the face of Britain! Then he got an offer to help change the face of Montreal, and I didn't want to go with him.'

'Why not?'

'I'd just started with Lister and Young, and——'

'You put your career before love?' Tariq's nostrils thinned.

'For a few years, yes. Anyway, he accepted the job without discussing it with me. Took it for granted I'd drop everything and do as he wanted.'

'So you split up?'

Stephanie shook her head. 'No. After he cooled down, he saw my point, but he'd already signed a contract and couldn't get out of it. Still, the salary was excellent, and we thought he'd save enough for us to get married when he came back.'

A pigeon fluttered around her hair, and she pushed it away, then threw more crumbs to the ground. She gave no sign of noticing Tariq's impatience to hear the rest. Let him stew a while!

'Such determined birds,' she remarked. 'They're worse than the ones in Trafalgar Square.'

'What happened when he got back from Montreal?'

Hiding her amusement, she flung him an ingenuous smile, deciding to let him suffer a little longer.

'I'd like another baklava, Tariq. They're the best I've tasted.'

Irritably he clicked his fingers for the waiter, and only when a plate of the delicious honey and almond confection was set in front of her did she answer his question.

'We'd both changed. The spark had gone.' Thoughtfully she bit into a triangle of pastry. 'I've often wondered if things would have worked out for us if I'd gone with him to Montreal, or whether we'd have grown apart anyway.'

'Hard to tell.' Tariq's voice was clipped. 'Personally I think absence makes the heart wander, not grow fonder!'

'With men more than women!'

His mouth quirked. 'I can't disagree there! We have a lower threshold of arousal.'

'Don't sound so pleased by it.' His answer annoyed her. 'Or don't you consider fidelity important?'

'Fidelity to what?'

'A wife, a girlfriend.'

'The two aren't the same—at least, not for *me*. I make no promises to a girlfriend. It's a sexual liaison and finishes when the sexual desire goes. But a wife is another matter entirely. There, one makes a promise and gives a commitment.' He folded his arms across his chest. 'But let's get back to you and your first boyfriend. You can't have had trouble replacing him.'

'I didn't want to. Jumping in and out of every Tom, Dick and Harry's bed isn't my scene.'

'You were waiting for the one-and-only?'

'I freely admit it. Even emancipated women can be old-fashioned!'

Tariq said nothing, and she had the distinct impression he did not believe her. But then he didn't want to. Far easier for him to contemplate seducing a girl of the world than one who held her virginity dear!

For the first time she admitted the possibility that his feelings for her had not deepened. Possibility? No, it was a certainty. For three weeks she had seen him almost daily, and he had never given a sign to show they were anything other than friends. She had taken a gamble and lost, and if she went on seeing him, she was in danger of jumping into his bed on *his* terms!

Dressing for her dinner with him later that evening,

Stephanie decided that, regardless of what he read into her action, this was going to be their last date.

The sound of his car brought her to the window and, forcing a smile to her lips, she leaned out and waved to him she was coming down.

No sooner did she shut the front door and see Tariq leaning nonchalantly against the bonnet, tall and urbane, eyes and mouth smiling as he watched her come towards him, then her resolution to part from him for ever dissolved like ice in boiling water. She loved him too much to walk out of his life!

Knowing that if she continued seeing him they would become lovers, and that every day of happiness would give her a month of hurt when they finally parted—she found it impossible to make light conversation on their drive to the restaurant.

'Anything wrong?' he asked.

'A headache,' she lied.

'Care to go home?'

'No thanks, I'll be fine. It's probably because I haven't eaten all day—other than an apple.'

'Wait till you've sampled Mehmet's *Sis Kebabi*. You'll soon be yourself again.'

Unfortunately she wasn't. For neither the kebab, the music and wine, nor their host's toothy hospitality managed to make her forget the problems ahead of her once she gave in to Tariq.

How would he behave when she did? Would he pretend he loved her? She hoped not, for she abhorred phoney emotion. He would be getting her on *his* terms, and was surely sophisticated enough not to try to deceive her.

Their journey home was silent, too. It was almost as if he was conscious of their having reached the crossroads in their relationship and wasn't certain which road she would take.

Stephanie bit back a sigh, acknowledging that the path she had chosen was a stony one leading to a cul-de-sac. She blocked her mind as to what might happen when she reached the end, or how long it would take her to get there. She couldn't very well ask him! How on earth could she put it without giving herself away?

'Tell me, Tariq darling, will our affair last a week, a month, a year? And when it's over, will we send each other Christmas cards and things?' She smiled at the notion, while tears made glittering spikes of her lashes, and she didn't move in case they overflowed.

'We must talk, I think,' Tariq pronounced as they reached the house.

She nodded and led the way up to her apartment, throwing her shawl on the settee, and moving into the kitchenette to switch on the percolator.

'Talk first, coffee later,' he murmured behind her.

Stephanie caught her breath. Here it was! Day of Nemesis: sword of Damocles dropping.

'Tariq, I——'

'Stephanie, I——'

Together they spoke, together they stopped.

'Let me speak first,' he said. 'I should have done when I called for you, and saved us both a disastrous evening.'

Her heart, pounding against her ribs, slowed almost to a stop. *He* was the one who was going to end it. He didn't even want an affair!

'I think you know what I'm going to say,' he went on.

Behind her the percolator bubbled, and she hurriedly turned to get the cups.

'Hear me out!' he ordered.

'I know it already.'

'Is turning your back on me your answer?'

'I don't have an answer.' She refused to face him. 'It's your decision and I can't fight it.'

'My dearest Stephanie,' he said softly, and swung her round to face him. 'I don't think you *do* know what's in my mind.' He muttered something in Turkish and shook his head. 'No, clearly you don't, and I've only myself to blame. I started out with a lie, and I assumed you knew it and were playing me along like a fisherman a merlin!'

Stephanie was scared to believe she was hearing correctly, and knowing the less said, the less given away, remained silent.

'I love you,' he said flatly.

Still she said nothing. Much as she had longed for him to say this, as a declaration it left a lot to be desired, and she sensed he had put up a tremendous fight with himself before making such an admission—which did not augur well for their future.

'I knew it the day you were nearly killed in front of me,' he went on, 'but I fought against it, persuaded myself it was nothing other than physical desire which I could satisfy by making love to you.'

'*That* part you made abundantly plain!'

'So was your answer! That's why I knew I had to be subtle: that I had to become your friend first and your lover later.' His grip on her tightened. 'And we *are* friends now, aren't we?'

'Yes,' she said, finding his honesty painful. Still, she had to admire him for it: admitting he loved her, yet making no effort to delude her it could lead to marriage! Having him set it out so precisely, made it all too easy to see the relationship they would have: a clandestine one that would come second to his public life, a public life in which she would have no existence.

'Where does Lala figure in all this?' she enquired.

A black eyebrow rose in a sharp arc. 'What does Lala

have to do with us?'

Well, that's certainly put me in my place, Stephanie thought bitterly, the particular place becoming more untenable by the second. So now she wasn't even supposed to mention the precious bride-to-be!

'I'm sorry if I've offended your sensibility by referring to her,' Stephanie snapped, 'but I've no intention of remaining your girlfriend after you're married!'

'I see.'

He drew back from her, his eyes hooded, his expression unreadable because of it. But she was strongly conscious of his amusement, and so angry she all but hit him. It might be fun for him, winning this game, but she would be the one to pay a bitter price.

'Do I take it you're prepared to have an affair with me *until* I marry?'

He was practically purring with satisfaction and Stephanie could not bring herself to say yes. But she had gone too far to say no, and all she managed was a nod.

'That should give us a couple of months, then.' His lids lifted to show the gleam of pleasure in his eyes. 'No longer though.'

The gall of him! Love and rage battled inside her, and rage finally won.

'No!' she stormed. 'I won't! I've changed my mind. Not even loving you can make me do it.'

'So you love me, eh?'

Too late she heard his triumph, and realising she had given herself away, was forced to brazen it out.

'Don't worry, Tariq, I'll get over it. I loved Freddy and I got over him, too.'

'That being the case, why can't we enjoy the next few months?'

'Because I've no intention of being your mistress until you take a wife!'

'Will you be my mistress until *you* become my wife?'

'You're the most arrogant, conceited . . .' She faltered haplessly. '*What did you say*?'

'You may well ask! I don't behave like the men in *your* world, Stephanie. I won't tell a woman I love her, then ask her to be my mistress!'

'You mean you're—you're asking me to marry you?'

'On bended knee if you wish.'

Tears gushed into her eyes, and she trembled with joy. She was still scared to believe it, but as she went on looking into the fine-cut face, no longer autocratic but filled with tenderness, she knew it was true.

'Bended knee isn't necessary, my darling. My answer's yes, yes, yes!'

Grinning broadly, he drew her close and pressed his mouth to hers. It was a kiss devoid of passion, an assurance of caring that gave her hope for their future. She was home at last, the still centre reached. So they stood together, suspended on a breath lest the spell be broken.

Inevitably it would be, as in all spells, and she knew their differences had to be discussed openly if their marriage was to work. It wasn't practicable to blithely ignore them.

Or was she worrying for nothing? Wasn't his proposal an acceptance of her way of life? As was *her* acceptance an admission that she would concede to his? In other words, compromise!

She bubbled with joy, and raising her head to tell him her thoughts, found his eyes on her, melting, luminous. Engulfed by his desire, she knew no panic as he gathered her closer still, only an overwhelming urge to give herself irrevocably to him, this man whom she loved with every fibre of her being.

She pressed closer to him, her body and hands telling

him what her tongue was too shy to say. Reading her gestures correctly, he groaned deep in his throat, then in one swift movement lifted her into his arms off the settee and strode with her to the bedroom.

Carefully he lowered her to the bed, then quickly undressed and came to her. He had not switched on the light and the full moon shone through the curtainless window, its rays gleaming on muscle and bone, on wide shoulders and narrow hips, on broad chest and flat, hard stomach.

He bent over her, and with swift, sure fingers, removed her dress. In brief lacy bra and satin panties, she lay before him, and his eyes roamed the swell of her breasts, her narrow waist and the curve of her belly that gave way to the long, pure line of her hips. Delicately his hands traced the same path, though they did not stop there but moved lower, searching below the clinging satin.

Unerringly he found the very core of her passion, his fingertips caressing the pulsing bud, arousing her to such mindless ecstasy that she reached for him blindly and pulled him on top of her. Her legs rose and twined around his waist, her body arching beneath his.

With an incoherent cry he thrust into her. Deep and sure, hard and high, penetrating her with the massive swell of his arousal. She gasped with the pain of it, but the pain was glorious, and her muscles clenched around him, gripping him in a vice of longing which had him moaning with need, his control lost as he thrust and thrust and thrust again, flooding her with the liquid of his life.

Together they travelled a spiral of ecstasy, spinning into a world beyond thought, a shimmering union of two bodies merging, two souls touching. They were suspended in blissful union, and when at last they moved apart and tremblingly returned to reason, they lay together exhausted, knowing they had experienced wholeness as never before, and would never experience it with anyone else.

'I love you so much.' Tariq's voice was still slurred with passion as he lay alongside her. 'I can't say you're everything I dreamed of because I never dreamed of such fulfilment.'

'Nor I.'

'Truly?' He raised himself on an elbow and peered at her in the darkness. 'I wanted to take it slowly, but seeing your body, feeling your skin on mine, I couldn't hold back.'

'I'm glad, or I'd have been there before you!'

He chuckled and ran his hand down her spine, curving his palm around her dimpled bottom. 'How pinchable it is!'

'Don't you dare or I'll——'

'What?'

She showed him, and his stomach muscles clenched with desire. 'God, you're asking for it!'

'You catch on quick!'

'You mean it?'

For answer she rolled on top of him. She bent forward to let her breasts, still damp from his tongue, undulate upon his chest, her nipples firing his.

His body jerked as though receiving an electric shock, and a sound, half-sigh, half-moan, escaped him. She lifted herself higher and he caught her shoulders and brought her back down on him, the movement so fast and hard he seemed to penetrate the very core of her. She writhed with wild abandon, filled with him, lost again in the all-pervading power of mutual climax.

'You've exhausted me,' he murmured, a long while

later, silky dark head pillowed on her breast. 'Drained me dry.'

'Strange. And *I* feel wonderful!'

A laugh rumbled through his chest. 'That's something else I love about you, my darling. Your humour, And an even bigger plus is that——' He stopped and ran the tip of his tongue over her ear.

'Is what?' she demanded.

'That you know when not to be funny!'

Her nails lightly raked a path down his spine and over the jutting bone of his hip. 'Like now?' she whispered.

'Like now,' he echoed, and once more slid into her. 'Easy does it, my lovely. I want this one to last. And when we've finished, don't move. I'd like to sleep inside you.'

'What a lovely idea.'

She felt him throb and swell, and languidly responded to it, her movements as delicate as his. Like a boat in a summer sea they rocked gently back and forth, slowly climbing the peak and staying there for endless, shimmering moments before returning to sanity.

'My dearest love,' he said huskily, and fell into instant sleep upon her shoulder.

'Carefully she inched herself into a more comfortable position and clasped her arm around his waist.

Holding Tariq, filled with Tariq, she was in heaven.

CHAPTER NINE

TARIQ left Stephanie at dawn, and dreamily she lay in bed and watched the sun rise in the pearly sky, its radiance as nothing to the radiance in her heart, or the glow that met her eyes when she caught her reflection in the bathroom mirror as she showered.

Tariq loved her and she was going to be his wife. It was incredible! Yet the long hours of loving they had shared, the aching tenderness of her breasts, the faint bruising on her inner thigh where he had gripped her, showed it was true.

She longed to share her happiness with someone, but her parents were cruising the Caribbean and her brothers mountaineering in Snowdonia. James was away, too—in England on annual leave—and she could imagine his astonishment when he heard. Also May's, when she returned at the end of the month.

'Maybe I'll climb to the top of the house and shout it from the rooftop,' she said aloud, and giggled at the notion. Life was marvellous and was going to be more so, a bubble of happiness that would expand and cover every moment of her life.

Donning one of her casual cottons, she stared longingly at the telephone, wanting to ring Tariq yet reluctant, for she had never called him at home. What if one of his family answered?

The thought of them caught her short, and a little grey cloud drifted on to her happy horizon. Not such a little one if she were truthful, for his family meant a great deal to him, his mother especially, and she was the one most likely to object to his marrying a foreigner, bearing in mind that she wanted Lala for him.

But family or no, it was Tariq's decision, and Stephanie was marrying *him*, not his relations. She hoped to have their approval, but if not, she was confident enough to live without it.

Even as she thought this, Tariq telephoned to tell her that he was taking her to see his mother that very day, and her entire confidence vanished. It was too soon, her happiness too fragile and new to be disclosed and bandied about.

But he was insistent—or his mother had been—that they come to lunch.

'She was delighted when I told her about us.'

'I wish you hadn't—not for a while, anyway.'

'Why?' he teased. 'Thinking of backing out?'

'No chance. I know when I'm on to a good thing! It's simply that . . .'

How to express her fear without sounding fearful? Besides, she didn't really understand what was bugging her.

'Mother's anxious to see you,' Tariq persisted.

'To inform me I'm not quite the girl she had in mind for her son,' Stephanie added wryly.

'No one, not even my mother, can tell me what to do with my life,' he affirmed. 'I love you and I'm going to marry you.'

In the event, Stephanie's misgivings regarding Mrs Hamid disappeared beneath her warm welcome, and she soon found herself completely at ease and able to enjoy lunch, which they ate in a small room overlooking a mosaic patio, where they retired for coffee.

No sooner were they settled when Tariq went to take a call from Paris, leaving Stephanie wondering if it was genuine or a ploy to leave her alone with his mother.

'I visit London quite often,' the woman declared, 'but I'm not familiar with the rest of England. I believe your parents live in the country?'

'Yes. In Buckinghamshire. They're both doctors and have a practice in a small village.'

'You have brothers and sisters?'

'Two brothers.'

'Married?'

'No.'

'So you'll be the first? I expect your parents are delighted for you. Though your mother must be sad, too.'

'Why sad?'

'Because you'll be living abroad.' Mrs Hamid's jewelled hands fluttered. 'A mother should be near her children. It gives her pleasure in her old age.'

'I don't think my mother will mind where I live,' Stephanie replied. 'She's used to my peripatetic life-style.'

'Are *you*? I mean, won't you miss moving around?'

'Not in the least. When you work in a country you tend to see only one part of it, and to be honest, one building site's much like another!'

The jewelled hands moved again, this time to pat the wings of silver on the black hair. 'Tariq hasn't said when you'll be marrying. I suppose you'll want to wait until the Clinic's finished?'

'I don't see why. The work's so advanced there's no necessity for me to be there every day. And Mustafa's more than capable of standing in for me while I'm on honeymoon.'

Mrs Hamid nodded. 'I'm glad to hear it. I'd be unhappy to think you were abandoning the project. We have such confidence in you, as you know.' Plump fingers busied themselves with the silver-gilt coffee pot. 'I expect your firm will be sorry to lose you.'

'Lose me?'

'You can hardly commute to London!'

Stephanie chuckled. 'I'm hoping to persuade John—Mr Lister—to open an office here. The Clinic will be a marvellous advertisement for us!'

Mrs Hamid's head tilted sharply, and sensing sudden disapproval, Stephanie realised where this conversation had been leading.

'I've no intention of retiring,' she stated positively, deciding to make a few things clear to her future mother-in-law. 'If John won't open up here, I'll do so myself.'

'You won't find that easy.'

'No harder than if I were setting up in England. Easier in fact, for I'll have Tariq's connections to help me.'

Mrs Hamid smoothed her silk dress over her well corsetted figure. 'It seems I'll have to get used to having a career girl for a daughter-in-law.'

'What's this about your daughter-in-law?' Tariq came into the room.

'She'll make a very lovely one.' His mother smiled indulgently at him as he went to sit beside Stephanie. 'Only you'll have to change your ideas, my son, and accept that you're going to have a working wife.'

'I've known that all along,' he said easily. 'Stephanie isn't the type to be satisfied with domesticity.'

He quirked an eyebrow at her. He was in fine humour, and it softened the curve of a mouth too often tight-set, warming eyes too often cold.

His mother smiled too, and as her eyes met Stephanie's there was something in them that showed her comment was not as guileless as she had tried to make out.

So what else was new? Stephanie thought cynically. I've thwarted her plans for her son, and it was naïve to expect her to welcome me, a foreigner, with open arms. Yet she had to play it cool for Tariq's sake. This was his mother, and it was better to have her as a friend than an enemy.

'Come, Stephanie.' Tariq drew her up with him. 'Time I showed you my apartment—and your future home.'

'But I—don't you live *here*?'

'Sure,' he drawled. 'In my own quarters, with my own front door key!'

His 'quarters' turned out to be a mansion within this palace—though knowing him as she now did, she didn't think it quite his style.

Astutely, he read her thoughts. 'You're free to make any changes here you like, my darling.'

'You should know better than to give an architect *carte blanche*!'

'Even when she's going to be my wife?'

'Especially!'

Grinning, Stephanie glanced round the living-room. The smaller of two, it was still huge by British standards, and she could see herself longing for some cosy den where they could sit together in the cool winter evenings.

'I think I *will* make some changes,' she confessed. 'But not until I've lived here a while and got the feel of the place.'

'If you'd be happier somewhere else, say so. Another house, or an apartment, if you'd prefer?'

'Oh no, I'd rather stay here. I love this garden, and when we have children they——'

She got no further, for he swung her into his arms and kissed her passionately.

'Hearing you speak of children,' he said throatily, 'is asking to be taken here and now!'

'What's stopping you?' she teased.

'I don't have a spare two hours!'

Laughing, she pulled away from him and snuggled into

an armchair. 'It will take some getting used to, living in a place this size.'

'You won't have to bother looking after it. We've plenty of staff.' He came to sit on the arm of her chair. 'I'm going to enjoy spoiling you, Stephanie. Giving you everything your heart desires, and some things it didn't even know it desired!'

'I only want you,' she whispered, catching his hand.

He drew her fingers to his lips, his teeth nibbling at them. He was more carefree than Stephanie had ever known him, light-hearted in manner as well as dress. His beige silk suit had the cut of Savile Row, but the jacket had been discarded, as had the Cardin tie, and his skin gleamed bronze through the fine cambric shirt. How well she knew his body, how intensely she longed to know it again.

'If you look at me like that,' he whispered, 'I won't be responsible for my actions. We'd better talk business.'

'If it's yours, you'll have to fill me in on what you do.'

'I'll be happy to.' He paused, smiling. 'Right now I'm planning on putting up some apartment blocks, which I thought you might like to design for me.'

She stared into his eyes, close enough to see the narrowed pupils and the warm brown irises surrounding them. They held no teasing glint, and the happiness she had felt all day, burgeoned until it threatened to overwhelm her.

'You're serious, Tariq?'

'Perfectly.'

Never in her wildest dreams had she imagined a plum like this falling into her lap. Fate was truly smiling on her!

'It's a bigger scheme than the Clinic,' he explained, 'and I've no objection to you bringing in Lister and Young.'

'I'd certainly like to discuss it with John.'

'Fine. The whole scheme should keep you busy at least until we start a family. After that, we can think again.'

Stephanie's ears pricked up. Think again about what? Did he see her profession as a hobby to while away the hours until the babies arrived, after which he expected her to settle into a world of nappies, nannies and more babies? She had always wanted a family, but had thought of having one in conjunction with her career, not instead of! Yet it sounded as if Tariq was throwing her a meaty bone to chew on until he put her in a maternal strait-jacket!

Anger engulfed her. He was being indulgent with her, acting as if he believed her hopes for her career had vanished the instant she had agreed to be his wife. Well, she had better put him straight!

'I plan carrying on with my career even when we have children. And nor do I intend relying on your largesse for work.'

'What largesse? My company can keep you busy for years. But if you'd rather look elsewhere, I'll engage someone else.'

Put like that, his offer seemed infinitely reasonable. Yet she still had doubts. 'What if the work dries up?'

'That's when you'll reap the benefit of having a husband to take care of you!' he chuckled.

As well he might, Stephanie thought sourly, for if he elected to call a moratorium on the Hamid Corporation's building projects—and they were her only client—she would be left high and dry as debris on a beach.

Her horizon, so clear and bright this morning, was filled with storm clouds threatening a deluge, and she was by no means sure how to stop it.

'Designing the apartment blocks is a marvellous opportunity for me,' she said swiftly. 'But I don't want to be solely dependent on you.'

'A wife *should* be dependent on her husband,' he declared. 'It makes him feel necessary.'

'We're discussing my work, Tariq, not our emotional involvement. If I had my own practice I'd have a greater sense of security.'

'*I'm* your security!' he said angrily. 'As my wife you'll have everything you want, and as an architect I'm giving you a fantastic opportunity. Yet you act as if I'm insulting you!'

'I'm not turning it down,' she pacified. 'I only want——'

'Everything your own way!'

'I could level that accusation at you.'

'Then you'd be wrong! My way would be for you to stay home, but I wouldn't even suggest it because I know you'd be unhappy. Yet when I offer you what I believe to be the ideal solution, you——'

'Ideal for you, perhaps,' she cut in. 'But you'd be taking away my freedom.'

'And replacing it with my love.'

Her scalp prickled, and she glanced at him. He had sat down again, this time in an ivory and wood carved chair, the back high as a throne, which she somehow thought fitting.

'What are you implying, Tariq?'

'That you can't be totally free when you love someone.'

'You're confusing the issue. My loving you has nothing to do with my profession. Where that's concerned, I must be allowed to choose my own clients—even turning *you* down if I wish! I don't think you can call that unreasonable. It's simply a question of compromise.'

'I've compromised to the point of generosity.'

Some generosity! If she did as he urged, he could pull the rug from under her any time he liked, and she'd be left holding the baby, figuratively and literally!

He was waiting for her to speak, and she was at a loss. Or maybe she had too much to say, and was scared that once started she wouldn't be able to stop. Yet to keep quiet was cowardly. They had reached the point of no return, and unless she could bring herself to travel his route, she dared not continue the journey.

She looked at him with anguish. He was standing by the window now, his broad frame against the sun, making him a silhouette that could have been anyone. But it wasn't anyone. It was Tariq, the man she loved, the man with whom she wanted to share her life. She longed to rush into his arms and tell him nothing mattered but their being together. Except that certain things did matter, and their marriage would fail if they did not see things each other's way, with no strings attached.

'Why are we fighting like this?'

The words were Tariq's, though they could have been hers, as he bridged the distance between them in a few long strides and pulled her close, his pent-up emotion spilling over as he buried his face in her golden hair.

'We mustn't quarrel,' he repeated thickly. 'It tears me apart.'

'Me, too.'

'We'll resolve everything, *sevgilim*—my darling, I promise you.'

She wished she could believe him, but logic told her that if she and Tariq weren't in accord today, they were unlikely to be in a month, or three months.

'We can't brush this issue aside,' she said. 'We have to settle it once and for all.'

Gently he drew her down with him on to the settee. 'If I didn't respect your talent, I wouldn't ask you to work for me, though I confess I've a selfish motive, too. You see,

I'm frequently away on business and I'd want you to be free to come with me whenever I can take you. If you're working for other people you mightn't be able to get away easily, and at the risk of offending your liberated views, I think your first loyalty should be to me.'

She had to hand it to him! Making out that wanting her professional freedom was being disloyal!

'I can't plan my life around your business trips,' she retorted.

'You must! I want first call on you.'

'I'm not your slave!' Angrily she jumped up. 'I have my own opinions, my own feelings!'

'And you wouldn't mind us being apart for months?'

'Of course I'd mind. But you don't go away on long trips. If you did, I'd obviously try to go with you.'

'What if you were in the middle of a big project?'

'Then I'd join you whenever I could.'

'That's a part-time marriage, Stephanie, and one I won't tolerate.'

'I won't tolerate yours, either!' she stormed. 'Seems to me you're only concerned with what *you* want.'

Her anger had brought her to the door, and she glared at him across the room, knowing they were both too het-up to make sense. They should cool down, go for a stroll in the garden perhaps. Unconsciously her hand fingered the door knob, and his eyes went instantly to it.

'Walk out on me now,' he grated, 'and *you'll* have to make the first move back!'

Startled, she realised he had misinterpreted her action. But instead of trying to stop her leaving, he was issuing another damned ultimatum.

'Well?' he said harshly 'What's it to be?'

'That's your decision, Tariq.' Turning her back, she walked out and slammed the door so hard behind her the walls trembled.

Once in the corridor she waited, heart pounding, for the sound of footsteps to tell her he was coming after her.

But the room remained silent as a grave, the door shut tight. Shakily she went down the stairs. Could it have ended so soon, this love she had thought would last for ever? Incredibly it had and, eyes brimming with tears, she reached the garden, slipped between the flowering shrubs to the road, and hailed a passing cab.

Never had Stephanie longed for a friend more than at this moment. But with May and James away, she had no one, and in an agony of lost hopes she paced the empty rooms of the old house, telling herself that even the greatest misery eventually eased.

Almost as if May were clairvoyant, a cable arrived from her next morning saying she would be home at the end of the week. Four agonising days to get through on her own. Stephanie almost turned tail and fled to England. Yet love for Tariq held her back; love and the conviction he wouldn't—couldn't—let them part like this. He was a proud man, she knew, and she had hurt him, but surely not too proud to compromise? And when he did, so would she.

Expecting her to work only for him wasn't really what she objected to; it was his chauvinist insistence that she obey him regardless that had enraged her. But now she had simmered down she recognised the benefit of having a 'boss' who was also her husband, though she would still insist on reserving the right to take on other projects if she found the Hamid Corporation too claustrophobic.

But the days passed without sight or sound of Tariq. Only James called to inform her he was back and when could they meet? The thought of making idle conversation with him was more than she could stomach. He knew nothing about her short-lived engagement—it had happened while he was on leave—and she was not about to confide in him. Pleading pressure of work, she promised to contact him the following week.

Luckily for her sanity, May returned Friday night, looking unusually smart in a Bill Blass suit. But the face was still devoid of make-up, the figure angular, the hair untidy wisps of pepper and salt.

'It's marvellous having you back!' Stephanie fell upon her and hugged her close. 'It seems like four months, not four weeks, and you look sensational.'

'Can't say the same about you,' May responded with characteristic bluntness, and ignoring the mound of luggage surrounding them, propelled Stephanie into the living-room. 'What have you been doing, dear girl? Working yourself to death? No, no, work never killed anyone. Out with it, then. What's going on?'

'Nothing. Everything's fine—c-couldn't be better. Oh, M-May . . .' Stephanie's lips trembled and she sank on to a chair and put her head in her hands. 'I don't know what to do!'

'First we'll have a snort of brandy,' May grunted, removing her jacket and going to the drinks tray to uncork a bottle of Remy Martin. 'It has to be a man, of course,' she muttered. 'And that means Tariq.'

Stephanie was startled. 'How did you know? I didn't realise it myself until three weeks ago!'

'I could have told you two months ago! You had all the symptoms.'

'I wish you'd warned me.'

'You'd have said I was nutty!' May took another sip of brandy. 'Your face tells me there's no happy ending.'

'I'm afraid so.'

'Care to get it off your chest?'

Wiping away her tears, Stephanie did. If she had hoped for comfort, she was disappointed, for May left her in no doubt that Tariq would never make the first move towards a reconciliation.

'According to his standards, he's gone incredibly far. He's accepted your desire to work, and given you the chance of doing so in his company. But you want jam on your bread as well as butter!'

'You know very well why I'm scared of being dependent on him.'

'You're not wrong.'

'Then why are you——'

'There are many ways of skinning a cat!'

'Feminine wiles?' Stephanie shook her head. 'Honestly, May, I never thought you'd suggest a thing like that!'

'I don't see why. We're all entitled to make the best of what we have! If we want to lead a donkey, we offer it a carrot not a stick! Not that Tariq's a donkey,' May grinned, 'but you get my meaning.'

'Loud and clear. But it's out of the question. I couldn't do anything so underhand.'

'Piffle! There isn't a man or woman born who hasn't at some stage used charm, guile, flattery, teasing, to get what they want. And if it doesn't hurt or destroy, where's the harm?'

'Stop making it sound so reasonable!' Stephanie couldn't help chuckling, even though she was denying the idea.

'But it *is* reasonable,' May persisted. 'What have you got to lose?'

'My self-respect. Anyway, say I married him believing I could change him, and then found I couldn't. Where would I be then?'

'In his bed at night and a darn sight happier than you are now! Apart from which, once you have a family, you mightn't want the hassle of your own practice.'

'All true. But at least I deserve the choice!'

'You've just made a choice. And damn miserable you are, too!'

'So is Tariq, I should think,' Stephanie sighed. 'If he could at least appreciate why it's important for me to feel free, I mightn't insist on it!'

May tugged at a strand of hair, a habit of hers when worried. 'If you're waiting for him to give in, so you can then be magnanimous and do the same, you'll have a long wait.'

'If he loves me, he will.'

'He's probably thinking exactly the same about you!'

Stephanie stared ahead. Every word May uttered was another nail in the coffin of her hopes. Yet to kid Tariq that she would accept his demands and then use guile to try to get her own way, was too underhand to contemplate. If their marriage couldn't be based on truth, she wanted no part of it.

Not surprisingly, Stephanie had a sleepless night.

It was obvious that if neither she nor Tariq budged from their opinions, they would never get back together. Yet she could not bring herself to make the first move—particularly if it were based on a lie. Apart from which, deep down she was convinced he would soon realise her demands were reasonable. She would give it a few days, and see what happened.

She was in the middle of breakfast—forcing down a piece of toast—when James called to invite her to dinner that evening.

Her first inclination was to refuse, but she had not seen him since his return from England, and it was rude to keep stalling. Besides, it was better to go out than sit staring at four walls, and James was amusing and uncomplicated to be with, which was exactly what she needed.

Being with another man might help her view her problems in perspective. She even toyed with the idea of confiding in James and asking his opinion, but quickly dismissed the notion as unfair. He had made no secret of being keen on her, and though discussing Tariq with him wouldn't exactly be rubbing salt in a wound, it would certainly be rubbing it on chapped skin!

Only as she dressed for her date with him did she appreciate why May had had a fit when she had seen her. She had lost pounds in weight and the hollows beneath her eyes gave them a soulful look which did not suit her normally vivacious personality. Not that she had been exactly vivacious this past week—a corpse would have been livelier company! Still, she had accepted James's invitation and had no intention of spoiling his evening by looking or acting like a mourner at a wake.

In the end she chose a 'little black dress' that did marvels for her complexion, and made her reflect whether it was so bad to be five pounds underweight, for she undoubtedly looked good enough to parade down the catwalk with the rest of the world's models. She smiled at the very notion. What boredom to be a clothes-horse, at the beck and call of fashion designers convinced that life began and ended with their creations! Still, they gave employment to thousands and pleasure to millions, so who was she to knock it?

Draping a scarlet taffeta shawl across her bare shoulders, she waited by the window for sight of James's car. A soft breeze wafted her hair, and she wished she hadn't worn it loose. Tariq liked this style, and each time she felt a strand brush her neck, it was almost as if it were his hand.

She glanced at her watch. Was there time to wind it into a coil? She was debating the point when a cheery toot on a horn made her look down and realise there wasn't. With a wave to James, she closed her window and ran downstairs.

He was standing by the car, and she was forcibly reminded that only eight days ago Tariq had done exactly the same. But *their* evening together had ended in her bed, with avowals of love and a happy future, whereas tonight . . .

Could she ever contemplate marrying James? At best, it would be a compromise. Damn that word! If it had been in Tariq's vocabulary, she wouldn't be here now, going out with someone who meant nothing to her.

'I'd forgotten how beautiful you are,' James greeted her, bending down to kiss her cheek.

All at once pride came to her aid. Let Tariq stew in his own juice! She didn't care if she never saw or heard from him again. He wasn't the only fish in the sea. Nor was she so old and ugly that she was unable to hook another one.

But all too soon her elation took a hard knock, for, entering the fashionable restaurant where James took her, she instantly spotted a broad-shouldered man with dark, brooding looks and a heart-stopping presence, dining with friends on the other side of the room.

Tariq! What nonsense he made of her contention that she would want to hook another fish, even if the sea were teeming with them! He was the only fish for her and she might as well admit it. And now she had, she could not allow things to go on in this nonsensical manner. They had to meet and talk. It was incredible that two intelligent people who loved one another should part over something that, with mutual willingness, could easily be resolved.

James, tall and blond beside her, was oblivious of the emotions raging in her as he gave his name to the *maître d'*, who immediately led them to a table.

It was uncomfortably close to Tariq's, and Stephanie

instantly went to sit with her back to him. But the waiter was already holding out the chair on the other side, and she was obliged to take it.

Quickly she picked up the menu and immersed herself in it as if her very life depended on it.

'If I'd realised you were starving,' James chuckled, 'I'd have called for you earlier!'

'Sorry, but I only had a sandwich for lunch.'

'How about a drink to stave off the pangs?'

'A Bloody Mary,' she answered, still not lifting her eyes.

'That's not your usual,' he said after he had given the order to the wine waiter.

'It's the mood I'm in.'

'The Bloody or the Mary?'

She raised her head slightly—she couldn't spend the entire meal with it lowered or James would think she was crazy—and said, 'Would it make any difference?'

'I'll say. Use your imagination!'

She did and blushed, then changed the topic. 'I'll skip a starter, if you don't mind, and go straight to charcoal-grilled lamb.' She set the menu flat on the table. She was no coward and she refused to act like one.

'I'll have the same,' James said, and as their drinks came, raised his glass to her.

She toasted him back, and lifting her head higher to do so, only had to turn her eyes a fraction to find Tariq's dark, amused ones looking directly at her, and refusing to move away.

She gave him the faintest smile, aware how stupid such formality was when he knew her more intimately than anyone. But how else to respond?

James looked over his shoulder to see who she was smiling at and, recognising Tariq, waved cheerily.

As if it were a signal, Tariq said something to his

friends, pushed back his chair, and came over to them.

He smiled briefly at Stephanie, then spoke to James. 'When did you get back?'

'A few days ago. And it rained throughout my leave!'

'Then you'll be glad of the sun.'

'I am.'

Banalities, banalities, Stephanie thought, with Tariq acting as if she weren't here, and James oblivious of anything untoward in the atmosphere.

'Things OK with you?' he asked Tariq easily. 'How's the Clinic going?'

'Stephanie can answer that better than I can.'

'Another month should see the major work finished,' she said coolly.

'Does that mean you'll soon be leaving here?' James asked.

'I'm not sure.' From the corner of her eye she saw Tariq tense, and hid her elation. He might have control over his voice and features, but not his body! 'It depends how soon John's mobile and can get out here to take over.'

'Would you like him to?' Tariq asked abruptly.

'Not really.' Stephanie forced herself to look at him. 'I've nursed this project through its teething troubles, and would rather like to be here till the teeth appear! But Mr Lister's the boss and he calls the shots.'

Tariq's shrug disclosed nothing, and with a cool 'goodnight' to them both, he returned to his table.

'What's with him?' James questioned. 'I've never known him so curt.'

'Was he? I didn't notice.'

She was delighted she could reply casually and hide her hurt that Tariq had treated her like a stranger. He was clearly telling her it was over between them. But it was unthinkable to sit back and watch their future together vanish without a fight. And if fighting meant talking, then so be it.

It required all her will-power to eat dinner when every mouthful she swallowed made her long to throw up, or to give her attention to James when every nerve-ending tingled with awareness of Tariq. But eventually the meal was over, the bill paid and they left the restaurant, with not so much as a glance from the black-haired man laughing and talking with his friends.

'I missed you when I was away,' James said as they drove home. 'You make the other girls I know seem stodgy as rice pudding.'

'What am I?' she teased. 'A soufflé?'

'Definitely not. They fall flat too quickly! You're lemon meringue pie. Sweet, yet excitingly astringent, with a frothy topping hiding a nice, firm base!'

She laughed. 'I'll never feel the same again about lemon meringue pie!'

'What am I?' he asked.

'Roast beef and Yorkshire pudding.'

'How ordinary!'

'On the contrary. It's something one never tires of.'

'That's the nicest compliment I've had in years!' He reached for her hand and squeezed it. 'I don't intend losing touch with you when you return home, Stephanie. We've something good going.' He stroked her fingers. 'You're not only lovely to look at, you're delightful to talk to!'

'A result of my working,' she said promptly.

'Could be.'

She swivelled in her seat to face him. 'Do you ever feel threatened by career women, James?'

'Threatened?' He was astonished. 'No, never. In my profession women rarely get to the top, anyway!'

'Only prime ministers,' Stephanie sniffed.

He laughed. 'Don't have a go at me, my angel. It's the system. When it comes to business, and especially the business of diplomacy, men prefer dealing with men.'

'How would you feel about your wife working?'

'Can't say I've given it any thought.' James drew to a stop outside her house but made no move to leave the car. 'Given the choice, I think most men would prefer having the "little woman" at home, cooking his food, taking care of his creature comforts. But if she isn't happy doing it—and many women aren't these days—one has to find a solution.'

'Just because a wife works, doesn't mean the home will suffer,' Stephanie retorted. 'It's quite often the opposite. If she earns enough they can hire help; if not, they can share the chores.'

'I agree absolutely,' he chuckled as he came round to help her out of the car, and was so clearly amused by the seriousness with which she had spoken, that she gave a sheepish smile.

'Sorry, James, but it's an old hobby-horse of mine, and once I mount it, I ride it hard.'

'Would I be wrong in assuming you once fell for a man who refused to settle for anything other than the "little woman"?'

'Something like that.'

'He was a fool, then.'

James bent to kiss her mouth. A light kiss that would have deepened had she not stepped back quickly to unlock the front door.

'May I see you again this week?' he called after her as she stepped into the hall.

'I'm not sure,' she called back. 'I'll be in touch.'

Feeling guilty, for it wasn't fair to lead James on, she decided to play it cooler with him in future. Not that she would need to once she and Tariq were together again. If only it were morning and she could go to him!

Anticipating another restless night—she was too excited to fall asleep—she none the less did the instant her head touched the pillow, and awoke to the usual bright sunshine filtering through the curtains.

She jumped out of bed, determined that before the sun set she and Tariq would have found a satisfactory solution to the problem of her career.

Determination lending her wings, she was dressed, breakfasted and downstairs within the half-hour, and was passing the hall table when a small package with her name on it caught her eye.

Puzzled, she picked it up and turned it over, then tore off the wrapping to reveal a small velvet box with a note attached. Trembling, she unfolded it, recognising the bold, heavy script from Tariq's signature on documents.

> 'My dearest one,
>
> How beautiful you looked last night, and how I longed to tell the world you were mine!
>
> When are you going to be sensible and accept that what I want is best for both of us? By being so obstinate, you are causing us both unnecessary heartache. I love you, my darling, and there'll never by anyone else for me.
>
> I hope you like the small token of my love—I've been carrying it around with me for days, hoping to give it to you personally, but I had forgotten there was a touch of red in that golden hair of yours! But oh, how I miss you and long to have you back.'

'On my terms' was what he hadn't added! Not that there was any need, for his message spelled it out loud and clear.

Grim-faced, Stephanie lifted the lid of the velvet box and saw an exquisite brooch of emeralds and pink pearls sparkling up at her from a cushion of midnight-blue satin. The 'token of his love'. The sum total it seemed, for it came without respect for her feelings, without understanding of her hopes, without appreciation of her need to be recognised as a person in her own right.

Nothing had changed! Tariq was as obdurate as ever; refusing to see her in terms other than a wife who would do his bidding.

Stuffing the jewel box into her purse, she hailed a cab to her office, and once there, rewrapped the package and asked her acting secretary to deliver it to Mr Hamid. That should tell him exactly what she thought of his gift and letter!

For the rest of the day she jumped nervously each time the telephone rang or the office door opened. But all that happened was a resounding nothing, and she returned home on tenterhooks, expecting him to be on the doorstep.

What she didn't anticipate was not seeing him at all, and by midnight her temper had cooled sufficiently for her to regret the haste with which she had returned the brooch.

She should have explained why his letter had infuriated her, then left it to him to decide if he wanted to go on defending his stance, or was prepared to meet her half-way.

If he didn't contact her within the next few days, she would pocket her pride and call him. Before receiving the brooch this morning, she had planned on doing it anyway, so she was only giving him the opportunity to make the first move.

When Friday dawned without his doing so, she decided to call him and invite him home.

Her hand was on the receiver when it rang, and shakily she raised it to her ear.

'Hi there,' said James, and her sense of let-down was dreadful. 'You promised to call and you haven't. So if the mountain et cetera, et cetera . . .'

'I'm sorry,' she apologised quickly. 'But the week's simply flown.'

'So has Tariq,' he quipped.

'I don't get you.'

'He's gone to the States. Left yesterday morning for a couple of months. I'm surprised he didn't tell you.'

She tried to speak but found it impossible. She had lost Tariq for good. She should never have sent back his present the way she had. He had seen it as an insult, as throwing his love in his face.

'You still there?' James asked.

'Yes, I—er—you've caught me at a busy time.'

'Not too busy to see me over the weekend, I hope?'

'Maybe Sunday. I'll be in touch.'

She put down the receiver, uncaring that she had been abrupt, knowing only that she would have burst into tears if she had continued talking. All she could think of was Tariq, and the devastating realisation that he had gone from her.

No matter how justified his anger or hurt, if he genuinely cared for her he could not have left the country without attempting a final reconciliation. The fact that he had made it clear beyond doubt that this was the end. Theirs was a love that had died almost as it was born, that had probably never had a chance to bloom, except in her own silly mind.

Accepting this Stephanie also accepted that she had to leave Turkey as soon as possible; leave this land of promise that had left its promise unfulfilled. She would call John and ask him to send someone to replace her.

When she had spoken to him the other day he had asked if she was happy to stay on, and she had said yes. But he would not think it odd if she changed her mind.

Only May put up an argument against her leaving.

'You can't blame Tariq for going off as he did. He may talk and act Western, but he thinks Middle Eastern, and if you love him, you'll accept the differences in your attitudes.'

'While he ignores mine?' Stephanie flared.

'He's had things his own way all his life, and you have to make haste slowly. I already warned you of that. Marry him, Stephanie, and *then* work at changing him.'

'I can't do that. It isn't honest.'

May raised her shoulders hopelessly, and their talk ended in stalemate, as it so often had for Stephanie these past few weeks.

Luckily for her frayed nerves, John posed no argument when she asked to be replaced, and within ten days sent out one of their junior architects to oversee the remainder of the contract.

That left only James, who accepted her departure with equal equanimity—possibly because his tour of duty in Istanbul was coming to a close and he knew he would soon be seeing her in London. Their relationship had not progressed further than warm friendship, but she knew it could, if she wanted. Trouble was, she didn't want; nor could she envisage letting another man come close to her.

She had only known Tariq a few short months, but it was as if she had loved him for ever and, though leaving here would not lessen her heartbreak, she dared not remain in a city where the very air she breathed, breathed of the man she loved more than life itself.

Still, she was young and resilient, and work would be her panacea. There were the retirement homes she was eager to get on to the drawing-board. With luck, she might even become a full partner in Lister and Young before her next birthday!

When that happened she would really know she had got somewhere, be a woman fulfilled ... It was marvellous!

So why did she feel as if her life was at an end?

CHAPTER TEN

STEPHANIE looked up from her drawing-board as her secretary came in with the mail.

'Hi, Janet. Anything interesting?'

'Not as far as I can see. Oh, there's a letter from Turkey.'

With an effort, Stephanie managed not to snatch at it, though the minute she had it in her hand and recognised May's writing, her expectancy died, and the familiar despondency returned.

Since coming home she had only had a brief note from May bringing her up to date with the gossip, and telling her Tariq was still in the States.

Slitting the envelope, she wondered if he was still there—it was three months since he had left Istanbul, how quickly time fled! She took out the closely written pages and settled back in her chair to read.

She didn't get beyond the first two lines, for May's opening paragraph told her the news she had been dreading, yet had braced herself to hear.

Tariq had married Lala!

Numb with grief, the pages slipped from her fingers. The one hope that had kept her going—that by some miracle she and Tariq would get back together—was shattered beyond repair.

She sat with eyes closed, trying not to absorb her misery, willing herself to let it wash around her and not penetrate her very bones. Inevitably it did, and tears rolled slowly down her cheeks. What price her career now? What price her life?

But that was defeatist thinking. She had known what she was letting herself in for when she had walked out on him and refused to go running back. And when Tariq had made no move to heal the breach she had still refused to compromise her principles and give in, accepting that if she did, she would regret it in years to come.

Now she had to pay the price of her independence and face the consequences. She must rebuild her life without him. Not an easy task by any means, but by marrying Lala he had left her no option.

Sighing, she retrieved the fallen pages and read on. They had married a week ago, May wrote, which meant Friday last. Stupidly Stephanie tried to think where she had been that day—or night! Poring over some dumb plans while Tariq and Lala ... Oh, it didn't bear thinking about!

Except that she could think of nothing else. All she could see was Tariq's bronzed body resting upon Lala's; his hands caressing the fragile bones, the shining black hair ...

Tears gushed into her eyes and she let them fall unchecked, knowing many more would follow in the months ahead.

Whatever might be said against hard work, there was nothing to beat it for keeping one's sanity, and Stephanie flung herself into it as if her very life depended on it, which—in the darkest hours of the night—she felt wasn't far short of the truth.

She was rewarded too, for John, quick to appreciate her efforts, made her a junior partner and put her in charge of their biggest project—building an international hotel on the Thames for one of the most prestigious companies in North America.

At last she had reached the top, where she had always

aimed to be. And how lonely Olympus was! How cold the rarefied air! She would get used to it, of course, and would soon find it exhilarating. It was only a matter of time. As was picking up the pieces of her life, which she had already begun doing anyway; working frenetically by day, dating frenetically at night and determinedly filling every single waking moment.

She was helped in this by James's return to England, and a temporary secondment to the Foreign Office. She was happy to see him once a week, but refused to let him commandeer as much of her time as he would have liked, fearing that if she did, he would read too much into it. She enjoyed having him as a friend but could not think of him as a husband. Could not see any man that way, other than Tariq. And he was lost to her!

She was sorely tempted to ring May, for she missed the woman's sharp mind and honesty. But whenever she went to call her, she chickened out, afraid May might think she simply wanted to glean the latest news of Tariq.

I'm mad to let him stop me speaking to a friend, she decided mutinously one morning, when she had a few moments to spare and was enjoying the unexpected pleasure of it. I'll do it this minute! Riffling through her diary for May's number, she reached for the telephone just as it rang.

'Stephanie?'

'May! What a coincidence! I was about to call you. Where are you?'

'In London, en route to the States. I'm leaving first thing in the morning. Is there any chance of our getting together? I'll understand if you're busy.'

'I'd cancel a date with the Queen to see you! Where shall we meet?'

'I'm at the Connaught.'

'Be with you in an hour.'

It was the best news possible. May, here! She hadn't realised how much she had missed her. Or perhaps it was because May was her one link with—dammit!—she must stop attaching Tariq to every event in her life.

Instructing her secretary to deal with all messages, she headed for the hotel.

May had only occupied the room for a few hours, yet already it bore the stamp of her personality: a mish-mash of books and magazines strewn about on tables, a silver-framed photograph of her beloved husband, a little filigree vase burning incense, the familiar smell of sandalwood that permeated May's home.

'It's great to see you again!' Stephanie cried, hugging her.

'There isn't that much to see of *you*. Any thinner and you'd pass for a stick insect!'

May drew away and blew her nose vigorously.

She hasn't changed a bit, Stephanie thought, regarding her affectionately. Still the same down-to-earth, forthright woman. So forthright, that hardly had they settled down to their drinks, when she made the pronouncement Stephanie had braced herself to hear from the moment she had learned of Tariq's marriage.

'Lala's expecting a baby.'

'Really? I'm amazed it didn't happen sooner.'

'One doesn't necessarily hit the jackpot first go!' came the dry response. 'Anyway, Tariq was taken ill on honeymoon—no one quite knows what with, some sort of virus, I gather—and he's only recently recovered. If he——' May stopped abruptly. 'Look, if talking about him upsets you, say so and I'll shut up. Except I think that psychologically it's better for you to know what's going on, rather than pretend he doesn't exist. At least until you don't give a damn about him any longer.'

'I doubt that day will ever come,' Stephanie whispered painfully.

'That's what I was afraid of. But you have to face facts, my dear. Tariq's gone from your life and won't be coming back into it.'

'Do you think I don't tell myself that every day? But it doesn't help.'

'Then be like Avis and try harder!'

'I can't try any harder,' Stephanie cried. 'Oh May, I can't believe it's over between us.'

'It is, dear girl. I'm afraid it is.' May's hand, cool and strong, rested momentarily on Stephanie's, and when next she spoke, she changed the subject entirely.

'See much of James?'

'About once a week.'

'Is he still keen on you?'

'Yes—which creates a problem. I like him too much to hurt him.'

'He's not a child, Stephanie, and if you don't raise his hopes . . .'

'I'm raising them just by going out with him!'

'He might grow on you, you know, and you could do worse. I like James. Always have.'

Stephanie remembered this next evening when, after going with him to a concert at the Festival Hall, they strolled along the Embankment and he unexpectedly asked her to marry him.

'*Marry* you?'

'Why so surprised?'

'Well, I—I didn't quite realise——'

'I was ready to pop the question?' He caught her by the shoulders and turned her to face him. 'I've been wanting to for weeks—months, in fact. I love you, Stephanie. Have done since the night I met you.' He feathered little kisses down her cheek to her lips. 'I only held off because

I wasn't sure how you felt about me. But tonight I decided to bite the bullet.'

He scanned her face, pale in the lamplight, and she tried to school her expression. But he read it correctly and gave a despondent sigh.

'Looks as if I bit too soon.'

She wanted to say he shouldn't have bitten at all, but did not have the heart. 'I'm sorry, James. But I—I'm not ready to marry anyone yet.'

'When you are, will I be in the running?'

'I don't know.' She heard his sharp intake of breath. 'I really am sorry,' she repeated, 'but I don't want to build up your hopes.'

'I wouldn't want you to.' In the overhead light she saw the grim set of his jaw. 'Is it anyone I know?'

'I—I never said there was anyone else.'

'But there is, isn't there? And it's Tariq, if I'm not mistaken.'

Miserably, she nodded.

'Stupid of me not to have realised it before,' he muttered. 'Those questions of yours about career women . . . That was to do with him, wasn't it?'

'Yes.' She tried to hide her agitation. 'Please, James, do you mind if we don't talk about it? It's pointless raking up something that's over.'

'I sincerely hope it is!'

'What's that supposed to mean?'

'That Tariq's married and you should forget him.'

'Which is why I'm here and he's there,' she rejoined with forced lightness, and though common sense told her to drop the subject, curiosity egged her on. 'What made you tumble to the truth, anyway? Did I give myself away or was it an inspired guess?'

'I'm not given to inspiration,' James said wryly. 'But there was always a tension between the two of you; the sort of emotion that leads to love or hate, rarely to indifference.'

Indifference. How she wished that word applied to her and Tariq!

'I'm sorry it couldn't have been you,' she sighed.

'So am I! And don't think I'm giving up on you, because I'm not!'

'Oh, James. I don't want to hurt you.'

'I'se a big boy!' he grinned. 'I can take care of myself.' He paused. 'May we still see each other?'

'Of course. But . . .'

'"Don't raise your hopes",' he finished ruefully. 'I promise I won't, so put your conscience back in cold storage!'

In the months that followed, James did not put a foot wrong, and Stephanie was glad of his companionship. Gradually she came to rely on him, even looked forward to seeing him, and had almost kidded herself she was getting over Tariq when she opened *The Times* one morning and saw his picture on the front page of the business section.

Her breath caught in her throat. She had forgotten how handsome he was! A little older-looking perhaps, with more than a sprinkling of grey at the temples. His expression was sombre, too, though this could be her imagination. Besides, it was a business photograph and he would hardly want to be portrayed as laughing boy! Quickly her eyes scanned the caption.

> 'Hamid International, one of the fastest growing companies in Asia, have recently opened a London office, and Mr Hamid, the president, who three months ago lost——'

My God! It couldn't be!

Heart racing, she read the caption again. Yes, it was true. She hadn't misread it. Lala was dead!

Slowly Stephanie lifted her eyes from the page. It must have occurred shortly after she had seen May in London. A miscarriage, probably. No wonder Tariq looked so sombre. He probably felt guilty for not having loved her.

Or had he? After all, what man, especially one from his background, could resist such an adoring, beautiful girl?

She pictured Lala as she had last seen her, a vision in blue at the musical soirée. Yet lovely though she had been, it was difficult to imagine Tariq falling in love with such a lightweight, and Stephanie was still convinced he had married out of pique.

Yet if that were true, why hadn't he called *her* once he was free, to find out if she was now willing to compromise?

There was only one reason why he hadn't, and with a despondent sigh she faced the unpalatable truth that he no longer loved her.

She was still trying to come to terms with this when James rang to ask if she had seen the article.

'I just have.'

'Poor Lala! She couldn't have been more than nineteen.'

'If that.'

'Seems Tariq's moving to London.'

'Only opening an office,' Stephanie countered. 'He has one in New York, too.'

'But he'll be coming here more often,' James said flatly, then added, 'Am I still seeing you tomorrow night?'

'Why not?'

'Just checking.'

'Don't be such a damned diplomat!'

Laughing, he rang off.

Amazingly, Stephanie managed to put Tariq completely from her mind for the rest of the day, though he haunted her dreams that night and made her welcome morning with open arms. If she didn't come to terms with her unconscious, she'd start wishing for insomnia!

She was musing on this as she crossed the lobby of Claridge's after a long and tedious meeting with a new client, when she heard a woman call her name.

Oh no! she despaired, swinging round. Oh yes, she acknowledged silently as her eyes came to rest on the smartly dressed figure of Mrs Hamid. Not quite the last person in the world she wanted to meet, but almost!

'Stephanie! I had a feeling it was you.'

'How nice to see you, Mrs Hamid.' She was disconcerted at how easily the lie tripped off her tongue, but consoled herself she was simply pandering to social convention. 'Here on a visit?'

'Yes. Tariq came here on business last week and I joined him yesterday.'

Last week! Any hopes Stephanie had cherished of him contacting her vanished on hearing this latest piece of information. If a few days had passed without his getting in touch with her, she would have understood it—put it down to pressure of work or embarrassed reluctance. But a week? No, she had to accept she meant nothing to him.

'I do hope you've time to share a pot of tea with me?' Mrs Hamid enquired.

Though the last thing Stephanie wanted was to prolong this meeting, there was no way she could politely get out of it, and with a calm that was only skin deep, she followed the woman into the aristocratic opulence of Claridge's lounge.

'You're looking very well,' Mrs Hamid said as they seated themselves at a small table.

'So are you, Mrs Hamid. How's Istanbul?'

What hard going this was! Stephanie knew she should

say something sympathetic about Lala, but was not sure how to broach the subject.

'I'm sorry you didn't call me before you left,' the older woman remarked. 'It made me feel you didn't regard me as a friend.'

'I didn't,' Stephanie said, deciding to hell with convention! 'I knew you didn't think me a suitable wife for your son, and I assumed you'd be pleased we parted.'

'Not because I didn't like you, my dear—there was nothing personal in it, I assure you. It's simply that I felt marriage between you would only end in acrimony. You were both too determined, too convinced your own way was right, to have been happy.'

'And who do *you* think was right?' Stephanie asked drily.

'My opinion doesn't matter! It's yours and my son's that count. And quite clearly you both had doubts, or you'd have married!'

How confidently Mrs Hamid spoke, and how simplistic she made it sound! Once again Stephanie realised what she had lost as oppposed to what she had gained. Yet if she could turn back the clock, she knew she would do exactly the same.

'I suppose you know our darling Lala died?' Mrs Hamid murmured, her eyes filling with tears.

'Yes. I read about it the other day. Was it—was it sudden?'

'Very. An aneurysm. One moment she was talking and laughing with Tariq, the next she was unconscious. It was a terrible shock for everyone. Such a tragedy.' The woman paused, hand shaking as she replenished Stephanie's cup and then her own. 'Tariq was inconsolable for months, but thank goodness he's finally realised life has to go on.'

'With another Lala' was implicit in everything Mrs

Hamid was saying, Stephanie acknowledged bitterly, and debated how soon she could politely leave.

'I must remember to take back some tea with me next week,' the woman deliberately went on to another tack. 'Though somehow it never quite tastes the same in Istanbul.'

'It probably has something to do with the water.'

'I never thought of that. You may be right.'

Relieved at the turn the conversation had taken, Stephanie firmly kept to banalities until she was finally able to make her departure a quarter of an hour later.

Only then did she give way to her misery, silently crying as she huddled in the back of a taxi and tried not to think that Tariq had been in London a whole week, walking the same streets as her, breathing the same air, yet hadn't thought to call her! But why should he? They weren't friends—simply one-time lovers!

Was I wrong to stand out for what I wanted? she agonised. Should I have done as May advised and tried to get my own way *after* I married him? Yet what if she had failed? She'd have had to give in to him, and sooner or later would have ended up despising herself for it. At least this way she had retained her integrity.

Drying her eyes, she sat up straight. It wasn't helping any to think of might-have-beens. The past was dead, long live the future! James was a far better bet for her. From here on she was going to be a realist and accept what was offered instead of wishing for what could never be.

She was glad she was seeing James that night. The last thing she wanted was to stay home and brood.

Sensitive to her mood, as always, he set out to amuse her and, warming to his kindness, she finally decided that next time he asked her to marry him, she would accept. They had masses of things in common and she liked him better than anyone else she knew.

By the time the evening had ended and he had left her in the lobby of her apartment block, she had almost convinced herself that becoming his wife was the ideal solution.

She had left the elevator and was nearing her front door when she sensed someone following her. Shoulder-bag at the ready to hit out, she swung round, the bag slipping from her nerveless hand as she recognised the man behind her.

Tariq!

Joy surged through her, and it was all she could do not to rush into his arms. A fig for Mrs Hamid's perception! He loved her and had come to tell her!

'Hello, Tariq!' Her tone—cool as a hostess to a gatecrasher—gave away nothing. 'I wasn't expecting you.' Well, that was true at least. 'Been waiting long?'

'Too long.' In the overhead light he looked pale and haggard, a shadow of the man she had fallen in love with. 'We must talk.'

'It's very late.'

'I've been here three hours.'

'Hardly my fault.'

Hell! Why was she acting as if he were a stranger when all she longed to do was hold him close? Yet he had married Lala, she reminded herself, and despite being free for months he hadn't come to her.

'May we go inside?' he asked raggedly. 'We can't talk here.'

Silently she unlocked the door and ushered him in, marvelling at how steady her hand was. Hardly had she closed the door when he gave a low groan and pulled her close, wrapping his arms around her as if afraid she would disappear.

With a sigh she rested against him, breathing in his

warmth, his scent. This was where she belonged; the light of her life was back.

'Better put on the light,' he ordered.

'Must we?' she laughed, wanting to tell him it already was.

He stretched a hand to the switch. 'I want to look at you,' he pronounced, cupping her face and ranging over it with his eyes. 'How beautiful you are! I'd almost forgotten.'

'Really?'

'No, I'm lying. I remember everything about you. Everything!' Gently he drew her into the living-room, and down on to the couch. 'I'll never let you leave me again, my dearest love. I swear it.'

Engulfed by his presence, she believed him. If she didn't she was lost.

'I'm sorry about Lala,' she whispered, and felt a shudder go through him.

'It was a tragedy,' he said heavily. 'She was so young. She had her whole life ahead of her.'

'With *you*?'

Stephanie hadn't realised that she had spoken aloud until her question echoed in the room. One part of her wished she could retract it, but the other didn't, for she knew it had to be said and, more importantly, answered.

Tariq knew it, too, for he drew back to look at her.

'Yes, Stephanie, with me. She was my wife, and had she lived she would have remained so.'

Icy tentacles seemed to riffle through Stephanie's hair, lifting it from her scalp. 'Then you were happy?'

'I love *you*.'

'That wasn't what I asked. Were you happy with Lala?'

'I'd come to terms with my marriage.'

'And would have spent the rest of your life with her? Forgotten me?'

'Never that! There wasn't a day I didn't think of you. Not a night I didn't ache to hold you in my arms.'

'Yet you stayed with Lala.'

'Yes.'

'And would have gone on doing so?' Stephanie reiterated, flagellating herself.

'Yes!' He almost shouted the word. 'Yes!'

If he had taken a knife and stabbed her, the pain couldn't have been worse. His loveless marriage had taught him nothing. He would have gone on with it rather than change his archaic attitude to women.

Bleakly, she stared at him. He had gone to stand by the fireplace, shoulders braced as if ready to take whatever verbal abuse she threw at him.

But she could say nothing! Speechless, she went on staring at him, conscious of what the past six months had done to him—the myriad lines fanning out from his eyes, the deeper ones marking either side of his mouth. But they did not detract from his looks—rather they lent him a greater sensuality. He was thinner too, the planes of his face clearly defined, making it easier to see the Tartar in him.

He's still a story-book hero, she reflected wryly; a man of any woman's dreams, providing the woman is content to follow him and not walk by his side.

'You should find another Turkish girl to marry.' Her cool tone gave no indication of the anger burning inside her. 'Our differences still exist, Tariq. In fact, there are more.'

'How can there be?'

'I'm thinking of your marriage.'

'It's over!'

'Only because Lala died.'

'I'd never break a contract,' he stated. 'My word is my bond.'

'So you'd have continued living a lie! Made love to one woman while your body yearned for another!'

He swung violently away, as if he could not bear to listen, his answer implicit in his action.

'I don't want you in my life on those terms,' Stephanie went on bitterly. 'That's not my kind of love.'

'What is, then?'

'One that can't be put in cold storage! What sort of person are you, that you'd have sacrificed your entire life—and mine, too—on the altar of a loveless marriage?'

'I'd have had no option if Lala were alive. I was the one who made the mistake, Stephanie, not her, and I couldn't have taken my happiness at her expense.'

'And making her happy at *mine* was OK?'

'It was your choice. I asked you to marry me and you walked out on me.'

'You made it untenable for me to stay!'

He flung out an arm. 'Why rake up the past when I'm offering you my future? You're using Lala as an excuse, aren't you?'

'An excuse for what?'

'To save you admitting you've made a new life for yourself with James!'

The words shattered into the room like stones through glass, and Stephanie couldn't believe she had heard him properly. He was white with fury, his mouth moving involuntarily, his hands clenching and unclenching. Hadn't he heard a word she had said, or was he so overcome by desire for her that he was deaf to reason?

Yet his question had given her a let-out—if she wanted to take it. She loved him, and would for the rest of her life. But Lala would always remain a running sore between them, festering, likely to erupt at any time.

Besides, the initial reason she had broken with Tariq was still unresolved. He hadn't even mentioned her career, or said anything to show he had changed his original, uncompromising attitude. So perhaps he thought *she* would!

Even as she debated this, he spoke again.

'I know it's James—so you needn't bother lying to me. You don't want a man, you want a lapdog! Someone who'll give in to your every whim!'

'As Lala did you?' Stephanie snapped.

'How right!'

'Then maybe she has a sister you can marry!'

With a muttered oath he stormed back to her and yanked her into his arms with a force that shook the breath from her body.

'Her sister's a child,' he ground out. 'Till she's older, I'll make do with you!'

That he meant it was evident from the brutality of his hold, the roughness with which his hands moved down her body.

Stephanie struggled against him, kicking out wildly. But she was a kitten fighting a tiger, and like a tiger he tore her dress from her in a violent movement that left her half naked in front of him, her breasts spilling from her bra, the clenched muscles of her stomach bare to his hot gaze.

'You're mine,' he panted. 'Mine—and I mean to have you!'

'Never! I'll see you in hell first!'

'I've been there already!' His hands marauded her, rough on her soft skin, and she clawed at him, trying to rake his face with her nails.

'I'll never let you take me!'

'You can't stop me.'

His mouth was hot on hers, stifling her cries as his

tongue thrust forward aggressively, mimicking the swelling organ pressing upon her thigh.

Only then did fear take hold of her, and she knew that nothing short of a miracle would stop him. And yet—treacherous thought—she didn't want him to stop!

His pillaging hands, searching out the hidden crevices of her body, were rousing her to a desire as mindless as his. She tried to resist it, but it was like stemming a dam. Waves of passion shivered through her as he touched the very core of her being, and with a sob she stopped fighting him.

How beautiful he was—sinewy muscles gleaming with sweat, the matt black hair on his chest curling damply round her twining fingers. When had he undressed? She didn't know or care, knew only that she wanted him, that her mouth hungered for the moistness of his, that her throbbing breasts ached for the touch of his fingers. The roundness of her belly was there to support him, and the burning heat between her thighs could only be cooled by the gush of his need for her.

Murmuring, crying, they fell to the floor, moonlight streaking their bodies as he mounted her. Together they ascended the pinnacle, the pinnacle that six months of longing made them reach too soon, coming together in a cataclysmic explosion that sent them soaring into a white heat of timelessness.

A long while later—or was it only moments?—Tariq lifted himself away from her, his face anguished.

'I . . . I don't know what to say.' His voice was a thread of sound as he hunched forward over his knees. 'If I could turn back the clock . . . If I could . . . Oh, God! Hate me if you want to, Stephanie, but it will never be as much as I hate myself.'

'I don't hate you, Tariq. I pity you.'

Bruised and shaken by his passion, she rose and

reached for her dress. Except that no covering could hide her shame, nor the burning anger she felt at being taken by force. Never mind that she had ended up responding to him. His initial onslaught could only be described in far uglier terms.

'You still haven't learned that possessing a woman won't make her yours,' Stephanie went on bitterly. 'She has to *give* herself to you, Tariq. She has to want you.' Reaction was setting in and she was finding it difficult to speak. Limbs trembling, skin burning as if with fever 'P-please go. There's no m-more for us to say . . . Nothing will change the situation.'

Silently he put on his clothes; zipping up his trousers, buttoning his shirt, slipping on his jacket. The naked, devouring man reverted to the sophisticate, and eyes—which moments ago had glittered with passsion—were blank as anodised steel.

He went to the door, and only when he opened it and was on the threshold, did he swing round to her.

'Try to understand, Stephanie. I've ached for you so much that I . . . You're a beautiful woman, all I've ever wanted, and when you rejected me I lost control.'

If he had used the word love, she might have run to him and damned the consequences. But to have him say he had lost control because she was a beautiful woman who had rejected him, turned her into nothing more than a sex object.

'Don't look at me like that!' he burst out. 'Can't you forgive me?'

'I'll do more than that, Tariq.' Stephanie forced her lips to curl in a mimicry of a smile. 'I'll forget you.'

CHAPTER ELEVEN

THE HOTEL on the Thames, which Lister and Young had designed and Stephanie was supervising, was such a huge project it left her little chance for brooding. No time for a social life either, for her American clients liked to be involved at every stage, which meant her jetting across the Atlantic so often she felt like a yo-yo. Indeed, had it not been for Concorde, she would have spent three-quarters of her life in an aircraft instead of only half!

But the continuous travel was taking its toll of her, if her increasing tiredness was anything to go by; and on this, her sixth trip to the States in five weeks, she felt so lethargic she was hard put not to lay her head on the glass and steel table in her clients' boardroom and fall asleep.

The gimlet eye of Ed Duggan, the chairman, was quick to notice it, and when the meeting ended, he rose and came over to her.

'I guess you think we're paranoid wanting to keep tabs on every detail?'

'I do rather! I can appreciate you watching over the financial side, but if you have confidence in my ability, you should leave *some* of the architectural decisions to me!'

The momentary stillness on his face showed he wasn't used to being spoken to this bluntly. But Stephanie was beyond caring. The constant chewing over of every minute detail was becoming intolerable, and if it went on, she would explode.

'You approved our designs and the contractors we engaged,' she said to the room at large. 'And I'd regard it as a sign of the board's confidence in me and my company if they allowed us to get on with the job!'

There was an electrified silence. No one had taken any notice when the chairman had gone over to speak to her, but as her voice rang out, the rest of the board members sat up and listened.

Now one of them spoke, a silver-haired gentleman whose Southern drawl hid a mind that made a rapier seem blunt.

'Miss Rodgers has a point, Ed. The glass-covered atrium in the inner courtyard, for example. We've seen three mock-ups of it, and had umpteen meetings to see if we want to go ahead with it, yet we still haven't reached a decision. As they say in my home state—if you have a good chicken, don't try laying your own eggs!'

'I'll check my diary and call a meeting to discuss it,' Ed Duggan stated.

Stephanie couldn't stop the giggle that escaped her, and the infectious sound rippled across the room, making her defender laugh and many of the others smile. Even Mr Duggan.

'I open my mouth and put my foot in it,' he said drily. 'Seems you're not wrong in your criticism, Stephanie.' He glanced from her to the man next to him. 'Nor are you, Tom. I suggest we appoint a three-man committee to liaise with Stephanie in London.'

This was considerably more than she had hoped for, and she was jubilant as she left the boardroom and walked down the corridor. She hadn't been as tactful as she might, but at least it had served to cut out these wearing transatlantic hops.

She drew a shaky breath. She felt faint and was glad she did not have to wait long for the elevator, though as she stepped inside it she couldn't help wishing it were less crowded.

Through a haze she saw the faces around her elongate,

shrink and elongate again, and she put out a hand to steady herself, gulping in air and longing to stop the elevator and rush out. It was zooming up and down as if gone mad—or else she was—and perspiration trickled down her face. She wrenched at the collar of her dress, gave a gasping cry, then sank into oblivion.

When she opened her eyes she was lying on a sofa in a strange room, with a stranger hovering over her. She tried to sit up, falling back as another spell of dizziness set the room spinning.

'Lie still,' the man ordered, putting a glass of water to her lips.

'What—what happened?' she asked shakily.

'You passed out in the elevator.'

Stephanie stared round the panel-lined office. 'How did I get here?'

'I carried you. I was visiting a patient on the sixth floor, and was standing next to you when you fainted.'

'You're a doctor?.'

'Nubar Ahmet.' He inclined his head.

He was every woman's idea of a doctor: tall, but not overwhelmingly so, with a black-haired, leonine head, eyes like coal, and a commanding nose above a firm mouth, the lower lip partially hidden by a neatly clipped black beard. The twinkle in his eye denied formality, the curl of his lip, any form of pomposity. Early forties, she guessed, and no shortage of women patients!

'Where do you live?' he asked. 'I'll take you home.'

Stephanie was grateful for the offer, for the room was still spinning. 'Thank you. I'm staying at the Plaza.'

'Very convenient. So am I.'

'You're not from New York, then?'

'No.'

He helped her rise, and she saw their eyes were level, though his muscularity made him appear taller. Not a general practitioner, she would bet, but a specialist of some kind, with an excellent bedside manner, if his solicitous guiding of her to a waiting cab was anything to go by.

'Forgive me. I'm sorry for not introducing myself,' she said as they drove along Park Avenue, 'I'm Stephanie Rodgers and I'm in New York on business.'

'Me, too.' If a voice could be described by colour, his was chocolate-brown, 'I'm attending a medical conference.'

'What's your specialty?'

A laugh rumbled through his chest. 'How American that sounds! I'm a psychiatrist.'

She asked him where he practised, thinking he could hail from anywhere east of Greece and west of China.

'In Istanbul,' he informed her.

Blankly she stared at him.

'Turkey,' he explained.

'Yes, I—I know it.'

He said nothing, and nor did she, relieved when the cab drew up at the hotel. To her surprise he went with her to collect her key, then, despite her assertion that she felt fine, insisted on seeing her to her room.

He hovered by the door and she wished he would go. All she needed was another Turk in her life! But he was only being concerned, as his next words proved.

'I advise you to get plenty of rest, Miss Rodgers. And a course of vitamins wouldn't come amiss either. In any event you should feel better in a month.'

'A month? I feel fine now!'

'You should still take it easy. Many women react as you do in the early stages of pregnancy, and——'

'Pregnancy?' Stephanie clung to the door, afraid she was going to faint again. A firm arm came out to support her, and the doctor took the key from her shaking hand

and inserted it in the lock.

'You didn't know?' he asked, fingers beneath her elbow as he led her in.

'No. Are you—how can you be sure?'

'Instinct. I may be wrong, of course, but if you aren't sure, I suggest you have a pregnancy test.'

Momentarily she closed her eyes. It was two months since she had seen Tariq; two months since . . . Her initial disbelief of what the doctor had told her was swamped by the certainty that he was right.

'I assumed women these days kept check of the dates,' he continued easily, perching on the arm of a chair.

'I usually do, but these last few months have been so hectic I didn't give it a thought.'

'Designing more clinics?'

She swallowed painfully, then with an enormous effort managed to say casually, 'You know the Hamid Clinic, then?'

'Yes. Tariq's a good friend of mine.'

'What a small world!' She aimed for, and achieved, a light laugh. 'I don't remember meeting you in Istanbul.'

'I was in Melbourne at the time. But I've visited the Clinic many times since, and Tariq's absolutely delighted with it.'

Stephanie breathed easier, for every word the good doctor said was thankfully marching him away from the truth.

'A pity you weren't there for the official opening,' he went on.

'Yes, it was,' she lied, remembering how angrily she had flung the invitation in the waste-paper basket.

'Maybe you'll come over and see it now it's functioning?'

'I'll give the building a chance to weather,' she smiled, relieved he was only linking her to Tariq professionally.

'Feeling better?' he asked.

'Much, thank you.'

'Then if you're not otherwise engaged tonight, will you give me the pleasure of taking you to dinner?'

She hesitated, strangely reluctant to accept, yet not knowing how to refuse without offending. 'What if I faint again?'

'Then you're definitely better off with a doctor to hand! However, I don't anticipate such a thing. If I'm not mistaken, Miss Rodgers, you had come from a lengthy meeting for which you'd prepared yourself with innumerable cups of black coffee and no food!'

'Spot on!' Stephanie chuckled. 'Did you say you're a psychiatrist or a psychic?'

'A bit of both!'

Hoping he would leave the psychic behind him when they dined together, she saw him to the door.

Alone, she stood in the centre of the room, fighting the sudden panic that threatened to overwhelm her. She was pregnant! What an idiot she was, not to have guessed this might be the outcome! But Tariq must never find out, even if it meant her going to the ends of the earth to hide it. And there was no question of her not having the baby. The idea of destroying the life they had created together didn't bear thinking of.

She would have to tell her parents of course, and she dreaded this more than anything. They didn't know about Tariq, and though her mother had guessed she had met someone special in Turkey, she had not asked any questions. But whatever her parents privately felt about the situation she had got herself into, she knew she could rely on their support.

Unexpectedly she remembered the offer she had received of a partnership in a well-established architectural firm in her home town. The idea of burying herself far from her friends and life in the big city had been too ludicrous to consider. Now it might be exactly what she needed: a safe haven in which to bring up her child and continue with her work. Except that there was less anonymity in a small town than in London . . . No, on second thoughts the country wasn't the solution. Besides, career-wise, it was better to remain with John.

Being pregnant would necessitate a complete change of life-style though. No jetting round the world on grandiose schemes with a slide rule and a bassinet! Fate had decreed she stay put for a while, and she had to plan her future accordingly.

All at once the baby took on a life of its own and, thinking of it inside her, she knew a moment of pure happiness that she was carrying part of Tariq. He had hurt her deeply, yet she still loved him, and fancifully wondered whether they had met in another lifetime. Only this could account for the sense of homecoming she experienced in his arms, for the peace as well as the passion he aroused in her.

She would devote her life to the baby's care and protection, and do everything in her power to ensure Tariq never discovered he was the father. If he did, he would demand a say in the child's upbringing—especially if it were a boy. He might even try to pressurise her into marrying him, which in a moment of weakness she might do! And that would only end in disaster, the ghost of Lala coming between them and destroying them.

An image of Tariq rose before her: olive skin, sable-brown eyes, midnight-black hair. It was unimaginable that a child of his would not have his colouring, and she could foresee the gossip and conjecture which would arise. But who cared! Let the world think what it liked; she would never admit the truth, except to her parents.

But this was in the future and, like Scarlett O'Hara, she

would think of it tomorrow.

First there was tonight, and dinner with Dr Ahmet. She was in too sombre a mood to wear anything dark, and chose scarlet silk that lent lustre to her pallor and sparkle to her eyes.

It brought an appreciative glint to the doctor's as she emerged into the lobby and found him waiting for her.

'I hardly recognised you,' he smiled. 'What a transformation! May I be let in on your secret?'

'It's between me and Estée Lauder!'

She marvelled she could be light-hearted. But why not? She had her health and strength, a marvellous career, and a positive attitude that should help her through the next trying months.

They went to a restaurant she had never been to before. Ethnic of course, this being the current trend, and Scandinavian, where they had gravidlax, and lamb in dill sauce, the whole washed down with excellent wine and conversation.

Nubar didn't refer to Tariq again, for which she was grateful, though she wasn't sure if he was being diplomatic or genuinely hadn't a clue how very nearly she had married his friend.

'You like music?' he asked as the waiter brought their coffee, it being one subject they hadn't touched on.

'Very much. Classics best. Especially Mahler and Mozart.'

'My favourites, too.' He was delighted. 'You play an instrument?'

'Not even a tin whistle!'

He laughed, and they continued talking music and musicians. From there it was a short step to art, a subject he was extemely *au fait* with. A man of many facets, she realised, and wondered if he were married, and if he allowed his wife to work.

'You're looking at me very quizzically,' he remarked. 'May I share your thoughts?'

'I don't see why not.' She told him them, and was rewarded with a grin.

'I've been married five years to a nurse who's now caring for our twins—six months old and bellows for lungs!'

'Any pictures of them?'

'None I intend boring you with! That's a vow I made the day they were born.'

'I wonder if I'll be strong-willed enough to do the same!'

Stephanie deliberately brought her unborn child into the conversation, to show him she wasn't running from the truth, and he tilted an eyebrow understandingly.

A little later, as they strolled down Fifth Avenue, with Central Park on their left and the Plaza Hotel looming ahead, he suggested they take a buggy ride.

'You're kidding!' she exclaimed. 'Where will we find one in New York?'

'Opposite our hotel. Haven't you seen them?'

'Would you think me an idiot if I said no?'

'I'd think you were working too hard to notice! So how about remedying it?'

'I'd like nothing better!'

He hurried her across the road to where three horse-drawn carriages stood, helped her into one, and asked the driver to take them round Central Park.

'Pity we can't dispense with the motor car,' he commented as they clip-clopped along sedately.

'You'd like that?'

'For the peace and quiet, yes.'

'Anything else you'd like to dispense with?' she asked.

'Meaning?'

'Would you be happy living in a bygone world?'

As she posed the question, Stephanie remembered Tariq asking her a similar one, and was suddenly so conscious of his presence, she would not have been surprised had he materialised. With a shake of her head, she pushed him from her mind.

'I'd quite enjoy going back in time for a short while,' Nubar answered her. 'But once the novelty had worn off I'd be impatient to get back to the twentieth century.'

'To tranquillisers and neurosurgery?' she joshed.

'And satellite communication, newspapers, antibiotics, lower infant mortality! Times change, and we with it.'

'Not always for the best.'

'What may not seem for the best one moment, may turn out quite differently the next.' Nubar swivelled round in his seat, the better to look at her. 'Tariq's in love with you,' he said unexpectedly.

Stephanie's breath caught in her throat. 'You certainly jump from one subject to another, don't you?'

'It's been on the tip of my tongue all evening.'

She said nothing, hoping he would change the subject again, though not surprised when he didn't.

'Tariq loves you, Stephanie.'

'He told you?'

'I'm his friend as well as his doctor.'

She played it cool. 'I understand he was ill soon after he married?'

'Yes, he was. Very.'

'He seemed fine when I last saw him.'

'That was after Lala died, wasn't it? He told me he'd seen you in London.'

No hint—either by word or gesture—that the good doctor suspected she was carrying Tariq's child.

'Did he also tell you he asked me to marry him and I refused?' Stephanie asked, deciding to be blunt.

'Yes. And I'm sorry you did. You mean more to him than any other woman.' The man hesitated. 'Unless of course you aren't in love with *him*?'

'I'm not.'

Nubar leaned towards her, his shoulder blotting out the Park, his hand tilting her chin and forcing her to meet his eyes.

'Would you consider me rude if I said I didn't believe you, and that I think you care for him very much indeed?'

'*Cared*,' she corrected. 'I stopped loving him when he married Lala.'

'He never stopped loving *you*. That was the trouble.'

'Trouble?'

Nubar straightened away from her and settled back in his seat. His face was in shadow but she sensed his tension, and guessed he was warring within himself.

'I can see why you were hurt by his marriage,' came the measured statement, 'but I assure you it taught him a bitter lesson.'

'Like hell it did!' Stephanie burst out. 'You obviously don't know him as well as I do. On his own admission he'd have stayed with Lala if she'd lived, so what price the lesson he learned?'

She waited for Nubar's denial, and when none came, said quietly, 'Thank you for not saying I'm wrong.'

'No, you're not wrong. But, on the other hand, it doesn't mean you're right.'

'Sounds like you're hedging your bets!'

'What I mean is that one shouldn't always believe what people say. Regardless of what Tariq told you, he would eventually have asked Lala for his freedom and come to you.'

'We'll have to agree to differ on that, I'm afraid.'

She braced herself for further argument, but none

came. The carriage moved along at a steady pace, the creak of leather and the wheels rattling along the road a soporific accompaniment to her thoughts. But unfortunately she could not put them to sleep. They remained alive and strong to torment her, and would do so for years to come.

'If you can't believe what I'm telling you,' Nubar said unexpectedly, 'do yourself a favour and talk to Tariq.'

'And get the same answer he gave me last time? No thanks.'

'It mightn't be the same.'

'Why will he have changed? Or would he just pretend he had, to satisfy me?'

'No, no. He may genuinely feel different.'

'*May*? I need a more positive answer than that to send me thousands of miles to see him!'

'I know exactly how he feels,' Nubar declared 'but I'm not sure if he'll actually own up to it. That's why it's important for you to see each other again. I love Tariq like a brother and I want his happiness as much as my own. But he'll only find it with you, Stephanie, so do us all a favour and go to Istanbul!'

Stubbornly she shook her head. 'I need a better reason than you've given me.'

'I can't say more. As his doctor, it wouldn't be ethical.'

'At least give me a hint.'

'I've said too much already.'

Stephanie's frustration grew. She had the feeling that many signs were being shown to her, but that she was too blind to read them.

'You've made me mistrust my judgement,' she cried, 'and now I don't know where I'm at!'

'I'm sorry.'

'So you should be! You can't leave me floundering like this, Nubar.'

'You're only floundering because you won't do as I say. If it's your pride that's holding you back, at least think of your child's future. Tariq's child.'

So he knew! She wanted to say it wasn't true, but as their eyes met, the lie died on her lips.

'I don't want him to find out, Nubar. Not ever.'

'You think that fair? Hasn't he the right to——'

'He forfeited any rights over me when he married Lala!'

'He was a free man when he came to you again and asked you to be his wife.'

'Physically free, not mentally. Oh, what's the use talking! Tariq and I are washed up.'

'Things aren't always as they seem.'

'That's the second time you've said that. I wish you wouldn't talk riddles!'

'I'm trying to make you solve them! No, no more questions,' he said as she went to interrupt him. 'The rest is up to you. See Tariq and force him to be honest with you.'

Tossing restlessly in bed that night, Stephanie wasn't sure she could. Such courage belonged to the brave; except what else to call having Tariq's child without his knowledge?

Yet did she have the strength of mind to put her love before her pride? For that was what it amounted to. The mere fact of going to Istanbul to see him would show him she still cared for him.

But what price pride if it meant a lifetime of loneliness?

CHAPTER TWELVE

RETURNING to London a week later, Stephanie had already made her decision. She would go to Turkey.

But going was the easy part. The difficult part was whether—once there—she would have the courage to face Tariq. Easy to think she would from the safety of her home and country, but when she actually saw him?

Only when she did, would she know, and the sooner she tested her courage the better.

Sitting across from John in his office, she debated how best to confess she was off to Istanbul for a few days. He had never questioned her about her relationship with Tariq, though from a few remarks he had made on her return, she was sure he had guessed she wasn't as indifferent to their client as she had made out.

Being John, he took her forthcoming departure in his stride, merely saying that it was an excellent idea for her to take a break, and why not stay a couple of weeks?

'Ed Duggan will have a fit if I'm away from his beloved hotel too long.'

'Forget Duggan.' John rubbed his hand across his grizzled hair, ruffling the short strands. 'You're part of Lister and Young, Stephanie, and if you were ill or otherwise engaged, someone else would take over from you. That's the benefit of not being a one-man band.'

He was making it easy for her to confide in him about the baby, and for an instant she wondered if he knew. Yet surely not. These last few weeks she had got thinner, not fatter, and short of his having X-ray eyes . . . No, before telling him she'd wait to see what happened in Turkey.

'You get my meaning?' John broke into her thoughts. 'I'm offering you a full partnership. I'll have the papers ready for you to sign on your return.'

'A full partnership?' In other circumstances she would have been delighted, but she was too emotionally muddled to think of anything beyond this moment.

'It's a marvellous offer, John, and thank you. But I'd like to think about it.'

If he was surprised she didn't jump at it, he was too astute to show it, and for the rest of their meeting they discussed the hotel and its problems.

A week later found Stephanie in Istanbul, once again at the Marmara. She telephoned no one, not even May. First, she had to see Tariq. Everything else was dependent on the outcome.

As soon as she had unpacked, she rang his office, but when the switchboard answered she dropped the receiver back on its rest. She couldn't talk to him in this faceless manner. She had to see him.

Only then did it occur to her that he might be away. Annoyed she hadn't ascertained this before coming here—a quick call would have done so—she nervously paced the carpet for several minutes before finally plucking up the courage to dial his number again and find out where he was.

The knowledge that he was barely ten minutes' walk away reduced her to such a mass of nerves that for the rest of the day she remained in her room, debating whether to do as Nubar had said, or take the morning plane to London.

A night of agonising decided her—maybe a few hours' restless sleep had unconsciously resolved her fears—and she jumped out of bed determined to see Tariq that very morning and damn the consequences.

Eleven o'clock found her a few yards from his office block, trying to rehearse what to say to him, and not knowing how or where to begin. She would play it by ear. See what his attitude was and take it from there. She neared the imposing marble edifice and stopped to draw a shaky breath.

Would he be glad to see her, or still angry that she had refused to marry him? If only she—oh God! there he was, coming through the entrance!

Her heart leapt at sight of him, but as she went to run forward, she saw the girl at his side. And what a girl! She could have passed for Lala's *doppelgänger*, except she was taller and, because of it, more striking.

Tariq apparently thought so too, if the affectionate way he was gazing at her was anything to go by. And as his arm came round the slender waist, and his dark head lowered intimately to the curly brunette one, Stephanie felt as if her life's blood was draining away.

Swiftly she drew back, intent on putting as much distance as possible between herself and this man. But her legs refused to respond to her brain, and like leaden weights they dragged her along the pavement. Sick with despair, she glanced over her shoulder and saw Tariq helping the girl into a waiting car, his tanned face lowering to let scarlet lips place a kiss on his lean cheek.

Only then did Stephanie regain command of her limbs, buoyed by anger at her stupidity for listening to Nubar. When had he seen Tariq last? A month at most, yet in this short time another woman had come into his life. No, not a woman, a girl, for she couldn't be more than twenty.

Blindly Stephanie pushed a path through the throng on the pavement, uncaring where she went as long as it was as far from here as possible. A group of people were coming towards her and, swerving to avoid them, she knocked into someone else.

Her handbag went flying and a furious invective was shouted at her in Turkish. Muttering an apology, she bent to retrieve her scattered belongings. Her hand was reaching out for her compact when a larger, darker one closed round it, and with an agonising sense of the inevitable, she raised her head and met Tariq's piercing eyes.

'You—you saw me?' she said stupidly.

'Only the back of you as you ran off.'

She groaned inwardly; her very action to avoid him had had the opposite effect. Gathering what pride she had left, she rose.

'I wasn't running off. I was—was having a stroll and suddenly realised I was late for an appointment.'

'Oh?' An eyebrow arched disbelievingly. 'With whom?'

'A client.'

'Anyone I know?'

'I haven't asked him.'

'You're not a very convincing liar. I think you're here to see me.'

Had it not been for the girl in the car, driving past them just then and giving Tariq a bewitching smile, Stephanie would have flung herself into his arms and cried, 'Yes, my darling, yes!'

'Come,' he stated, rising with her and taking her firmly by the arm.

'Where to?'

'Home. We have things to say to each other.'

'*I* haven't.'

'You came to Istanbul to say nothing?'

He was smiling slightly as he spoke, then as she

watched, his face tightened as if with anger, as did his grip on her arm.

'We're past this kind of prevarication, Stephanie. I've no intention of letting you go until I know why you're here.'

Before she could argue, he pulled her none too gently to the kerbside, hailed a passing taxi and pushed her in ahead of him.

It was a short drive to his house, and she was glad the noise of traffic prevented them talking. Not that she was in any mood for conversation. All she could think of was the girl she had seen with Tariq, and how stupid she had been to come here.

As the graceful façade of his home came into view, she all but jumped from the cab. Seeing Mrs Hamid would be the last straw, for that was taking her pride and stamping on it.

'What's wrong?' Tariq demanded, noticing her agitation.

'Can't we go somewhere else to talk?'

His eyes narrowed to slits, and red stained his high cheekbones. 'You'll be perfectly safe—no matter where we are. I promise not to touch you.'

Matching colour flamed into her face as she realised he had misunderstood her. But no way was she going to explain she hadn't wanted to meet his mother, and silently she followed him from the cab.

To her relief, he took her round the side of the house and through an arched courtyard to a carved door that gave access to his private quarters.

Entering them, she was instantly cast back to the few hours of their engagement, and wondered how different their lives would have been if she had married him and accepted his plans for her career. But the past couldn't be changed, nor the future it seemed, for someone else was already in it.

So what? a little voice questioned inside her. He still wants *you*. It's on his face when he looks at you, in his trembling hands when he touches you. You can easily make him forget this other girl. Go close and let him breathe in the scent of you . . .

But Stephanie refused to move. She had no intention of letting sex bring them together. There had to be more. Besides, the fact that he had found someone else so quickly revealed the shallowness of his emotions.

So immersed was she in her thoughts, she was unaware of going through the various rooms to reach the book-lined study where he had brought her the first time she had come here. Only as he shut the door behind him with an ominous thud did she admit she had a few tricky moments ahead of her if she wanted to leave here without disclosing her reason for coming.

'What a super room,' she chattered brightly, glancing at the carved ceiling, magnificent Turkish rugs and spendid ivory inlaid desk and chair.

'I'm glad you like it.' His tone was dry. 'But I didn't bring you here to discuss the décor. You came to Istanbul to see me, and I want to know why. And don't give me any rubbish about a client!'

'Very well.' She spoke quietly, her mind racing. 'I did have a reason, but—but somehow when I came here and saw you it was no longer valid.'

Her answer semed to take him aback, and she watched him ponder on it. That he didn't like it was obvious from his frown, and she was congratulating herself she had managed to fox him, when he said, 'You're trying to fob me off, Stephanie, and I won't have it, I want the truth.'

'I've given it to you. If you don't believe me, that's your problem.'

'Yours, too.'

'What does that mean?'

'That you'll stay here till you answer me.'

'As your prisoner, I suppose? How archaic!'

To hide her trembling legs, she sank on to a leather pouffe embossed with green and gold thread, and did her best to look uncaring.

If only she hadn't listened to Nubar, and rushed across Europe to confront a man who was quite content to put her out of his life!

Yet 'content' was the wrong word, for if she had found him changed two months ago, there was a bigger change in him today. The hollows beneath his cheekbones had deepened, the shadows under his eyes darkened, and the flecks of grey at his temples were two silver bands. Whatever hell he had put her through, he had gone through one of his own.

'I gather you met Nubar at a dinner party in New York,' Tariq said unexpectedly.

She tensed, trying to guess what else Nubar might have said, and comforting herself that medical ethics wouldn't have allowed him to break a patient's confidence by disclosing that she was pregnant.

'He thought you beautiful and intelligent,' Tariq went on, 'and said I was insane not to fight for you!'

'People change,' she shrugged.

'I haven't, and never will.' His tone was deep, husky, as if coming from the very depths of him. 'There'll never be another woman for me—only you.'

'Even when you remarry?'

'It will be you, or no one.'

She opened her mouth to reply, then closed it. He saw the movement, and the sombreness in his eyes vanished, making them glitter with their usual brilliance.

'You've jumped to the wrong conclusion, I think,' he chided.

'Conclusion?'

'About Yasmin—the girl you saw me with.'

'I haven't given her a thought.'

'I'm happy to hear it. None the less I'd like you to meet her. She's getting married next month and I'll see she invites you to the wedding.'

'How could you——'

'She'd never say no to her favourite uncle.'

'Uncle!'

'Yes. I hope that teaches you not to prejudge me?'

'Oh Tariq, I'm so sorry.'

'So you should be!' he grinned.

Stephanie was flooded with such joy she couldn't think straight. Her hands came out to him, and in two strides he was beside her, pulling her up and enfolding her in his arms; holding her so close that she heard his heart pounding in her ear, his breath rasping in his lungs as he muttered 'I love you,' over and over again.

'And I love *you*,' she cried, knowing the time had gone for prevarication. This was Tariq, father of her child, the only man she would ever want, and she wanted him to know it. 'I love you. I always have. I always will.'

His hands moved down her body, skimming her spine to cup her buttocks and press them so close to him that she felt his hardening thighs. Her mouth parted to drink him in, and his thrusting tongue answered the movement, tasting the moist sweetness she offered and replenishing it with his own. Her breasts swelled with arousal, pushing against the hard wall of his chest until he eased away and his hand came up to enfold them, his fingers gently rubbing her throbbing nipples. Desire spasmed through her, and with a gasp she caught his hand and pulled it away.

With a soft laugh he let her, but as his arm lowered, his hand moved the silken folds of her skirt and found a more vulnerable resting place between her legs.

'Tariq!' she gasped as questing fingers parted the heated flesh and touched the pulsing bud. 'Tariq, I can't . . .' Another spasm shook her and she clutched at him, her legs incapable of holding her.

Fiercely he pushed her on to the ottoman, coming down with her and covering her body with his. She gasped at the weight of him, and he instantly rested on his elbows, his face above hers, his eyes glazed with passion.

'I need you' he said thickly. 'You're the meaning to my life, the only reason I'm living. Without you I'm a husk.'

'It's the same with me.'

'Then why have we wasted so much time?'

Urgently he parted her legs, but even as he did, she flattened her palms upon his chest and held him off.

'Not yet. We must talk.'

'Talk!' he said thickly. 'Crazy woman! All I want to do is——'

'No, Tariq! Please . . . there's so much to say.'

'We've said everything that's important. We love each other. That's all that counts.'

Wishing she could agree, she slid from under him and stood up. She pulled down her skirt, straightened the bodice of her dress and smoothed her hair, conscious all the while of him watching her, a slight smile lifting the corners of his mouth.

'What wonderful creatures women are,' he teased, 'One moment hot as curry, the next cool as ice!'

'I'd love a long, cool drink!' she said mischieviously, and followed him with loving eyes as he went to a carved cabinet and opened it to disclose a refrigerated interior stacked with fruit cordials, white wine, champagne.

'The man with everything!' she laughed.

'Now that *you're* here, yes!' He came across to her with a frosted glass. 'Rum punch,' he explained, seeing her eye it.

'I didn't really want alcohol.'

'I put in very little. It's more of a rum tickle!'

Smiling, she sipped. 'Hmm, delicious.'

'So are you. But before I tell you how delicious, I think you should tell me why you came to Istanbul.'

He was so close that the fragrance of him filled her nostrils. Desire dissolved pride, and it was easy to be completely honest.

'Nubar said if I loved you, I should——'

'What about James?'

'James?' She blinked at him. 'You don't seriously think I'd marry *him*?'

'Why not? A few seconds ago you seriously thought I'd marry Yasmin!'

'That's different. You had your arm around her and you were—dammit, Tariq! I never gave you any reason to think I cared for James.'

'*He* did,' came the dry response. 'We dined together the night before he returned to London, and he made it plain he included you in his future. Which you rather endorsed when I asked you about him that night in your apartment.'

'Only because I was furious with you for thinking it! Anyway, I was using him as a shield.'

'Your shield, but my dagger.'

Stephanie winced at the pain in his voice. No wonder he looked as if he'd been to hell and back!

'Lala was mine,' she confessed. 'She still is.'

'Darling, don't! The poor girl's dead.'

Although Stephanie felt dreadful about it, the thought of the child she was carrying forced her to speak.

'You want me to be honest, and I will. I can't forget what you said to me in London. That if Lala were alive, you'd still be with her. It makes me feel you only see me as someone you come to for—for . . .' Unable to go on, she lowered her head.

With a muttered oath, Tariq flung away from her, his movements jerky as his voice. 'There are so many things you don't know. Things I—I can't talk about. But I love you. Not just for your body, Stephanie, but because with you I'm a whole man, fulfilled in every way.'

It was too impassioned a statement for her to disbelieve, but he still hadn't answered the pertinent question; and until he did, she'd have no peace.

'But if Lala——'

'Let her rest!'

'I can't until you've answered me!'

His mouth moved convulsively, as if he had trouble speaking. But he had no need to, for his expression said it all. Realising her journey had been futile, she set down her glass and went to the door.

'Where are you going?' he demanded, striding over to her.

'Home. Nothing's changed for us. I shouldn't have come.'

'You can't walk out on me! Forget Lala,' he pleaded. 'She's in the past.'

'Not for me, she isn't. Don't you see that? Your past is *my* present, Tariq. Everything you've said proves that what you felt for her was stronger—and still is—than your feelings for me.'

'That isn't true!'

Inexorably she opened the door.

'Stephanie, wait! I can't let you go. Not again.' He barred the way, his skin shiny with perspiration, his eyes wild. 'I know how you feel and I don't blame you for it.

But—but things aren't as they seem.'

Nubar had said almost the same and she hadn't understood him any more than she understood Tariq.

'Stop playing games with me!' she cried. 'I'm not in the mood.'

'I'm not playing games. I'm fighting for our happiness.' He propelled her back into the room. 'I can't let you go. I can't destroy *you* as well as myself—and that's what I'd be doing. I see it so clearly now.' He drew a shuddering breath. 'I've lived a lie because I didn't have the courage to admit that some tragedies can't be avoided. But one tragedy can—your leaving me.'

Incapable of going on, he turned away from her, and though Stephanie was mystified, she realised she had accidentally opened a door he had been keeping tightly shut.

But though it was now ajar, the rigidity of his body showed what an effort it was for him to push it open and disclose what lay behind it.

'Shall I come back later?' she asked softly.

'No, darling. Stay with me. I have to tell you the truth.'

CHAPTER THIRTEEN

STEPHANIE made herself comfortable on the ottoman by the window. Although afraid of what she was going to learn about Tariq's marriage, she had to hear him out. After all, she had come here for that very purpose.

Silently she watched him take the ornate chair behind his desk. Magnificent though it was, it did not diminish him; rather the opposite, for the curved back outlined his broad shoulders, and his strong hands rested on the arms, regal and impressive.

'It's damnably hard for me to begin,' he muttered. 'The more so because I wasn't honest with you in London.'

He paused, still at a loss, and Stephanie knew he was battling with himself. His hands were gripping the arms of the chair, his knuckles pale as the ivory, and her heart went out to him. If only she could say, 'I don't want to know. The past doesn't matter!' But it did—very much indeed.

'I'm seeing things differently now,' he went on, his voice low, almost as if he were speaking to himself. 'I couldn't tell you the truth in London because I felt I was being disloyal to Lala's memory. But just now, when you were going to walk out, I knew the living had to come before the dead, and that I owed *you* my loyalty.' He stopped again, then burst out, 'Lala never suspected how I felt about you. She believed I loved her.'

This wasn't what Stephanie had flown thousands of miles to hear! Yet she had asked for the truth, and could hardly complain because she was getting it!

Reading her thoughts, Tariq sighed. 'Don't jump to

conclusions, Stephanie. Wait till you know the whole story.' He rubbed the side of his face wearily. 'Lala didn't find me easy to live with. I was moody, bad-tempered, cold—but she put it down to my illness.'

This was the first mention he had made of being ill, though the little she had gleaned from May and Nubar made her pretty sure it had coloured his behaviour. She waited for him to elucidate, and when he didn't prompted gently, 'May wrote to me that you weren't well, but when I saw her in London she said you were fine.'

'Fine enough to function on a business level, perhaps, but emotionally I was a zombie, living in a nightmare of depression.'

Depression! Stephanie was staggered. Tariq was so strong and confident, this was the last thing she had imagined him suffering from.

'What caused it?' she asked.

'My marriage. My stupid intransigence. You see, it never entered my head you'd go back to England without giving us another chance to talk things over. And when I returned from the States and found you'd gone, I was so furious I proposed to Lala the very same night! Which was the biggest mistake of my life!'

'Pity you didn't realise it before you married her,' Stephanie rejoined.

'I was too damn full of pride to realise anything. It was only on my wedding night that——'

'For heaven's sake, Tariq!' Stephanie clapped her hands to her ears. 'There's a limit to confession!'

'Not to mine! You've got to hear me out! That first night, when Lala fell asleep in my arms, I realised I'd made the biggest mistake of my life. Making love to her had been nothing more than an act on my part, and——'

'Stop it!' Stephanie shouted. 'I don't want to hear!'

'I can't stop now. You asked for the truth, didn't you?'

His hand banged down on the desk, trembling the inkstand, the silver-framed photographs. 'After that first night, I couldn't touch her again. If it couldn't be you, then it couldn't be anyone. Do you know what I'm saying, Stephanie? I was impotent—impotent!'

Once again he had staggered her, and she tried to absorb what she had just learned.

'For days I battled with myself,' he went on huskily. 'But it was hopeless. I couldn't even share Lala's room, let alone her bed! How's that for a loving bridegroom!' His smile was a tormented grimace. 'Poor child, I can't tell you what it did to her. She was distraught, convinced it was her fault, and nothing I said could reassure her. It was a nightmare for us both, and for two months I lived with her tears, her pleas . . .'

Tariq raised his head and looked at Stephanie, his face so lifeless that it could have been a death mask. Her heart went out to him but she knew better than to speak.

'Then I had a breakdown,' he said into the silence. 'I couldn't talk, couldn't even think—Lala was finally happy.'

Stephanie blinked. 'Happy?'

'She was able to blame my behaviour on my illness, instead of the other way round!'

Tariq leaned back in his chair and closed his eyes. The lids were bruised with fatigue, and she stifled the urge to run across and gather his head to her breast, knowing that now he had unleashed his control, it was cathartic for him to go on speaking.

'Nubar counselled me for weeks,' he said quietly. 'But I couldn't take in anything he said. All I knew was that I'd made a prison for myself and couldn't escape from it without dishonouring my family. I know it's hard for Westerners to appreciate how we Turks feel about such things——'

'But I do,' Stephanie cut in.

'Then perhaps you can understand what I was going through! I couldn't tell Lala I didn't love her, yet I couldn't be a proper husband to her, either! So I took flight into depression. It was my alibi—my get-out!'

Impatiently he jumped to his feet, keeping the width of the desk between them, as if not trusting himself to be near her.

'It took weeks for Nubar to make me see I either had to work at my marriage or ask for my freedom. But I finally realised that even though it meant abandoning beliefs I'd considered immutable, I couldn't live without you.'

Stephanie's eyes filled with tears. 'If only I'd known what you were going through!'

'It was no more than I deserved.' He gave a heavy sigh. 'The one thing I'll always be thankful for was that Lala never guessed what I'd decided to do.'

'You mean——'

'Before I could tell her, she told me she was expecting a baby.'

'Oh, Tariq!'

It required little imagination for Stephanie to guess he must have felt enclosed in a steel trap. So many things fell into place, so many puzzles were resolved, questions answered.

'I'll never forget how happy she was that afternoon,' he said sadly, 'though I felt I'd been condemned to a living death. I couldn't believe that one night had destroyed my future with you. But it had, and I was forced to play the happy husband even though I knew I could never be the loving one.'

'I'd have understood it if you had been,' Stephanie said swiftly.

'I couldn't be. Though luckily Lala was too happy about the child to give it any thought. Then suddenly she was dead. One moment we were talking about names—the next she'd collapsed in my arms, her eyes blank.'

As if he too were blind, Tariq groped for the chair and sat down. 'She never regained consciousness, and died later that night. Poor little Lala . . . I felt as if I'd killed her; as if my wish to be free had made it happen. That's why I didn't come to you straight away. It was my punishment, you see.'

For a split second Stephanie was too startled to speak. Then she did, vehemently. 'That's crazy talk! Your mother said it was an aneurysm; she could have been born with it.'

'You're being logical,' he said wearily, 'and at that time I could only function emotionally.'

'Didn't Nubar——'

'He'd gone to Australia again.' Tariq raised his head, the sunlight catching the glitter of tears. 'For months I forced myself to stay away from you, but eventually I couldn't fight any longer, though I gave myself the excuse of opening a London office.'

'If only you'd told me the whole story then!'

'I tried, but . . . I was so happy to see you again it made my guilt worse! Then when you asked if I'd have remained with Lala if she'd lived, I couldn't bring myself to say no. I felt that if I did, I'd be burying her all over again.'

'That was crazy thinking!'

'I know.' His voice was barely audible. 'But it was the way I felt.'

Stephanie ran over to kneel beside him. 'You don't need to say any more, Tariq. Forget it now.'

Tentatively he put out a hand and stroked her hair. 'I put you through such hell,' he whispered. 'But I'll do everything in my power to make up for it.'

He said no more, and nor did she. The silence

lengthened, the only sounds coming from outside: the distant rattle of an old car, the mournful hoot of a ferry.

At last she knew why Nubar—wise to the working of the human mind—had urged her to see Tariq again. And he'd been right! She knew that remorse, not adherence to tradition and family honour, had impelled Tariq to say he would have remained Lala's husband had she lived.

So why aren't I over the moon? Stephanie asked herself. Why do I have this flat, empty feeling? She was searching for the reason, knowing there had to be one, yet not knowing how to find it, when Tariq spoke.

'When I remember how I forced myself on you that night . . . God! for weeks I could barely live with myself. I wanted to beg your forgiveness, plead with you to give me another chance. But I was scared.'

'Of what?'

'Of your disgust; that you wouldn't forgive me. As long as I didn't know for sure, I could still hope. But if that had gone . . .'

'Then it's a good thing I took the initiative,' she smiled, and all at once knew why she wasn't overjoyed. Because Tariq hadn't come to *her*. Because if she hadn't made the first move, they'd still be apart. Might have stayed apart for ever!

'You beat me to it by a day,' he said wryly, his eyes lightening with amusement. 'This time tomorrow I'd have been in London.'

'Truly?' Was he saying it because he sensed it was what she wanted to hear?

'See for yourself.' He pulled open the drawer of the desk and took out an airline ticket. 'An undated return, I might add, because I intended staying with you until you came back with me!'

Flinging herself into his arms, Stephanie smothered his face with kisses, murmuring broken endearments which he finally stopped with his lips.

She responded passionately to their touch, giving herself over to the pleasurable feel of his body, the sensual scent of his arousal. She caressed the silky hair, her fingers lingering on the nape of his neck as her tongue rubbed against his in ever-quickening movements until, with a groan, he pushed her away.

'Stop bewitching me. I've more to say.'

'Can't it wait?'

'No.' He caught her roving hands. 'The reason you left me—you were right, my dearest. I knew it myself as soon as I'd cooled down, but I was too pig-headed to admit it. And by the time I was ready to, you'd gone.'

'I——'

'You can open a hundred offices,' he cut in, 'and build houses all over the world, if that's what makes you happy!'

'It doesn't. Not any longer. You're my happiness, Tariq. That's something I've learned, too. So if the offer of working for Hamid International is still open . . .

For an answer he gathered her closer, and Stephanie, resting against him, thought of the child she was carrying and longed to tell him. But not now. Later tonight . . .

'When will you marry me?' he asked.

'As soon as you get the licence.'

'Good.' His voice was deep. 'I won't rest easy till you've signed on the dotted line.' He tilted her face to gaze into her eyes, and with a happy cry she hugged him tight.

'My soon-to-be husband,' she crooned. 'I can't believe it.'

'Nor can I.' He spoke without raising his mouth from hers, his breath warm on her lips. 'My soon-to-be-wife—who'll always be her own woman!'

MAIL-IN-OFFER

OFFER CERTIFICATE

I have enclosed the required number of proofs of purchase from any specially marked "Gifts From The Heart" Harlequin romance book, plus cash register receipts and a check or money order payable to Harlequin Gifts From The Heart Offer, to cover postage and handling.

002

CHECK ONE	ITEM	# OF PROOFS OF PURCHASE	POSTAGE & HANDLING FEE
	01 Brass Picture Frame	2	$ 1.00
	02 Heart-Shaped Candle Holders with Candles	3	$ 1.00
	03 Heart-Shaped Keepsake Box	4	$ 1.00
	04 Gold-Plated Heart Pendant	5	$ 1.00
	05 Collectors' Doll Limited quantities available	12	$ 2.75

NAME ______________________________

STREET ADDRESS ____________________ APT. # ______

CITY ______________ STATE ________ ZIP ________

Mail this certificate, designated number of proofs of purchase (inside back page) and check or money order for postage and handling to:

Gifts From The Heart, P.O. Box 4814
Reidsville, N. Carolina 27322-4814

NOTE THIS IMPORTANT OFFER'S TERMS

Requests must be postmarked by May 31, 1988. Only proofs of purchase from specially marked "Gifts From The Heart" Harlequin books will be accepted. This certificate plus cash register receipts and a check or money order to cover postage and handling must accompany your request and may not be reproduced in any manner. Offer void where prohibited, taxed or restricted by law. LIMIT ONE REQUEST PER NAME, FAMILY, GROUP, ORGANIZATION OR ADDRESS. Please allow up to 8 weeks after receipt of order for shipment. Offer only good in the U.S.A. Hurry—Limited quantities of collectors' doll available. Collectors' dolls will be mailed to first 15,000 qualifying submitters. All other submitters will receive 12 free previously unpublished Harlequin books and a postage & handling refund.

OFFER-1RR

PAMELA BROWNING

... is fireworks on the green at the Fourth of July and prayers said around the Thanksgiving table. It is the dream of freedom realized in thousands of small towns across this great nation.

But mostly, the Heartland is its people. People who care about and help one another. People who cherish traditional values and give to their children the greatest gift, the gift of love.

American Romance presents HEARTLAND, an emotional trilogy about people whose memories, hopes and dreams are bound up in the acres they farm.

HEARTLAND... the story of America.

Don't miss these heartfelt stories: American Romance #237 SIMPLE GIFTS (March), #241 FLY AWAY (April), and #245 HARVEST HOME (May).